"Max?" Kitt Whispered.

"It's okay," he whispered back. "It's a girl. And she's fine."

"Are you sure?"

"Positive."

"Could I see her?"

"Just hold your horses for two seconds, princess. I kind of have my hands full. She needs some cleaning up, but that's a little tough to do when all I've got to work with are some clothes I swiped from your suitcase. I'm afraid you're going to need a whole new wardrobe after tonight."

"I want—*need*—my daughter, Max."

He stopped talking. Kitt felt the soft, light weight of the baby he laid on her breasts. She could barely make out the soft fuzz of blond hair, the scrunched red face, one tiny squeezed fist no bigger than her thumb.

She had the crown of the baby's head nestled under her cheek when she looked up at Max. His eyes held her in a rich, savoring bond. "You did it honey."

"*We* did it," she said. "Thank you."

Dear Reader:

Welcome to the world of Silhouette Desire. Join me as we travel to a land of incredible passion and tantalizing romance—a place where dreams can, and do, come true.

When I read a Silhouette Desire, I sometimes feel as if I'm going on a little vacation. I can relax, put my feet up, and be transported to a new world . . . a world that has, naturally, a perfect hero just waiting to whisk me away! These are stories to remember, containing moments to treasure.

Silhouette Desire novels are romantic love stories—sensuous yet emotional. As a reader, you not only see the hero and heroine fall in love, you also feel what they're feeling.

Look for books by some of your favorite Silhouette Desire authors: Joan Hohl, BJ James, Linda Lael Miller and Diana Palmer.

So enjoy!

Lucia Macro
Senior Editor

JENNIFER GREENE

SLOW DANCE

SILHOUETTE *Desire*

Published by Silhouette Books New York

America's Publisher of Contemporary Romance

SILHOUETTE BOOKS
300 East 42nd St., New York, N.Y. 10017

ISBN: 0-373-05600-1

First Silhouette Books printing October 1990

Printed in the U.S.A.

JENNIFER GREENE

lives on a centennial farm near Lake Michigan with her husband and two children. Before writing full-time, she worked as a personnel manager, college counselor and teacher.

Ms. Greene has won many awards for her category romances, and was most recently named an RWA Golden Medallion Finalist and the *Romantic Times* Best Series Author of 1988-1989. Nineteen ninety marked the publication of her fifteenth romance for Silhouette Books. She has also written as Jeanne Grant.

One

In the summer months, only two things could keep Max Carlson awake past midnight—a willing woman and money.

For the past few years he'd had the good sense to avoid all women, willing or otherwise, and considering that right now he was hot, sweaty, starved and blinding tired, the issue was moot. Sex was the last thing on his mind.

Money, however, was a dependably enduring motivator.

Blinking the sandy grit of the road from his eyes, he shifted gears. His aging ten-wheeler wheezed up another rolling hill, and he checked his cargo in the rearview mirror. The load he was hauling was worth two thousand bucks—hardly a fortune, but it was his first cash flow of the year. He needed every dime of it.

The pallets of plump, pretty peaches sat on his truck bed, glowing in the moonlight. The fruit looked as sturdy as big blushing baseballs, but it wasn't. Nothing was more fragile than a peach. Max grew twelve varieties, and this first of the season—Garnet Beauty—was even more temperamental than the rest. A Garnet demanded more attention than a spoiled woman. Talk to 'em mean and they bruised. They had to be cosseted and babied and nurtured, and even then they were a risk.

His front tire hit a pothole. Max winced—not for himself but for his babies. The night was black as a demon, and the winding country road was completely unfamiliar to him. Normally he marketed his peaches closer to home, but his usual buyer, Litowski, was being a shyster about the price.

Max had once been the laid-back type. He'd lost that flaw in his character when his ex-wife took him to the cleaners four years before. Now he gave nothing away for free—the twist of acid in his stomach was a constant reminder that this farm season could make or break him—and for an extra two bucks a bushel he'd have delivered his babies as far as Poughkeepsie.

Stifling an exhausted yawn, he only wished he really were in Poughkeepsie. The potholed excuse for a road was worse than a wilderness. He hadn't seen another car since he'd left the main highway. Moonlight caught the shine of tangled, dew-sticky brush, leading to impenetrable woods on his left. To his right were dunes. The mountains of ghostly white sand that ultimately led to Lake Michigan were eerily still. Now there wasn't a house or light in sight. Occasionally his headlights caught the gleam of animal eyes.

It was a good place for spooks and ghost stories. Max just wanted his cash, followed, as soon as possible, by a shower and the nearest mattress. It was rarely this hot on the coast mid-July, but tonight was a humid blinger. His shirt stuck to his spine; his nape itched with peach fuzz; and his muscles ached after a seventeen-hour workday.

He groped on the dash for a chocolate bar—he always kept a stash for the days he didn't have time for dinner—but all he found was a dusty wrench and a spray manual.

His stomach growled just as the truck creaked up another hill. When it crested the top, Max immediately noticed the car. The white Le Sabre looked new, freshly waxed and abandoned, but that wasn't what captured his attention. Its tail end jutted a few inches in the traveling lane, and its engine dipped low on the narrow shoulder. No one parked like that. Even a stalled car should have been pushed off the road.

In deference to his peaches, his speed already rivaled a poke-slow turtle's, but he slowed down even further as he passed the car. He caught a moonlit gleam of pristine white upholstery in the empty driver's seat and the bulk of something dark in the back. Maybe that something moved.

And maybe you're so tired you can't see straight, he told himself. His gaze looked into the rearview mirror. There was no way he was going to stop. He didn't have time. The broker was waiting for his peaches; he was dead on his feet, and he had another full day of work starting in six hours. There was no flare, no driver trying to flag down his help. This was just a deserted car. The cops would find it. It wasn't his problem.

But thirty yards down the road Max pulled over, irritably jerked the gear into reverse and backed up the truck. Life had zapped any do-gooder instincts out of him years ago. Max considered himself cynical, tough and callous. And he'd go right back to being cynical, tough and callous—as soon as he was positive no one was in the back of the car. Sticking out as it was, the Le Sabre's left fender could be rammed by anyone taking the last hill at any speed.

He snatched a high-powered flashlight and climbed out of the truck. A mosquito nailed his neck before he even had the door slammed.

With the engine turned off, the only sound in the still night was the crunch of his boots on soft gravel. Not a leaf stirred in the deserted vale, which was why the hair rose on the back of his neck when he heard a sudden sound. A spooky, animal sound. A sound as primeval as pain.

His stride quickened to a jog until he reached the car. One glance reaffirmed that the expensive white leather seats in front were empty. The car's windows were open in front, closed in back. Moonlight created a double reflection on the pane; he couldn't see anything until he bent down. The single beam of his flashlight illuminated a body huddled in the back seat and a woman's pinched white face—and then she screamed.

The woman had lungs on her that could curdle milk. He'd never meant to scare her, yet the shriek of fear was oddly reassuring. Maybe she was in pain, but if she was strong enough to scream that loud she couldn't very well be dying. "Take it easy, take it easy. No one's going to hurt you. My name's Max Carlson, and if you'll look out the window, you'll see my truck. I'm just a farmer. I only stopped because it looked like you were in trouble."

At the same time he was talking, he averted the flashlight beam and yanked at the door handle. It was locked. Why the fool woman would bother locking the doors when the front windows were wide open was beyond him, but he didn't waste time sweating it. Unless he was mistaken—he hoped to God he was mistaken—he could smell the faint, too-sweet scent of blood. He whipped an arm through an open window and pushed up the back-door lock, then twisted around and wrenched the door open.

Stifling hot air poured out. Inside, the smells of blood and sweat were incongruously mixed with the scent of a woman's spicy, expensive perfume. The back seat was too shadowed for him to see clearly, but she was half-lying on her back and all twisted up. "Where are you hurt and how bad?" he clipped out.

"I need...I need an ambulance." Her eyes closed and she made another of those sounds—a blind, helpless sound that made his skin chill from the inside out. "My name is Kitt...Sanders. My purse is in front. You can take anything I have if you'd just... drive for a phone. Any phone. Please? I need a doctor."

He didn't doubt that, but without knowing what was wrong with her, he couldn't determine if she also needed immediate first aid. He ran the flashlight over the length of her. She tried to bat the bright light away, but he saw enough to make his throat close.

Like her car, she was all in white—classy slacks and a silky top—and he caught the glint of pricey gold at her wrists and throat. The trappings were affluent, all the symbols of success that his ex-wife had revered, and Max's defensive reaction was automatic. It also didn't last long. Affluence wouldn't help the kind of trouble she was in. Her clothes were soaking wet, her white face shining with sweat and her eyes wild with panic and fear—and his flashlight showed the reason.

Her stomach was as big and round as a watermelon.

He murmured a pithy four-letter word under his breath. "Do me a favor and tell me you're not in labor."

"Go away."

"You're bleeding. How bad?"

"Leave me *alone*. Please! If you're willing to help, for God's sake, go find a phone. That's..."

She couldn't finish the thought before another cramp ripped through her. On his fortieth birthday the month before, Max had noticed a trace of silver in his sideburns. Somehow he had the feeling he was going to turn completely white before this night was over. "Dammit, how often are those coming?"

"They don't...stop."

"For how long?"

"Forever."

"I don't suppose you could be a little more specific?"

"Look, mister...Max...whoever you are." Maybe another time her voice would be a whiskey-laced-with-honey alto. Now it was parched and scared and angry. "I really don't have time for idle conversation.

Maybe you haven't figured out that I'm having a hell of a day. First the air conditioning goes out in my car, then the car quits altogether in the middle of nowhere, then these contractions started. The baby isn't due for three weeks. I'm not supposed to be in labor. It's a hundred and ten degrees. I've been bitten by every mosquito from here to Chicago, and as far as I know I'm going to die—"

He hated to interrupt her monologue but it was necessary. "You're not going to die."

"Whether you can believe it or not, right now I'm not sure I care—and either way it's not your problem. The only possible way you could help would be to hightail it out of here for the nearest telephone..." Her voice rose on the pitch of a four-letter word he rarely heard a lady say. She strung it out like a singer belting out the last note in a ballad.

It couldn't have been a minute and a half since her last contraction. Max had the trapped sensation of a leaf being sucked into quicksand. She obviously didn't want a stranger near her. He didn't blame her, and her plea for him to "hightail it out of here" struck him as a delightful idea.

Delightful, but not viable. He backed out of the car and took a long bleak look at the deserted road. The nearest hospital he knew was in St. Joe. He could reach the twin cities of Benton Harbor/St. Joseph in a half hour with a fast car—only he didn't have a fast car. With his ten-wheeler loaded with peaches, the drive could easily take an hour. If her contractions were coming that fast he was scared she wouldn't make it, and leaving her to find a phone struck him as even more dangerous. He didn't know the road, had no idea where the nearest phone was. Even assuming he managed to rouse someone in a farmhouse, there would still be a wait for an ambulance while she was stuck alone.

Of all the lucky men who could have been passing by, why did fate have to pick him? And he could smell his peaches ripening in the sultry night heat. His broker was waiting with a hydracooler, and they'd start to spoil in a matter of hours without it. He thought irritably, You owe me for this one, God.

Whining about spilled milk, of course, accomplished nothing. Sliding into her driver's seat, he groped for the slit that held her car key.

"What . . . are you doing?"

"The obvious—taking one problem at a time. And the first thing we have to do is get this white princess off the road before someone coming over that hill slams into your fender."

"The car won't run."

Of course it would. Max didn't pay any attention for the obvious reason. Both the look of her—and her car—carried the gold-edged label of city slicker. She wouldn't know anything about mechanics. Max could take an engine from a scrap heap and make it hum— the Lord knew he had enough experience—and full of confidence, he turned the key.

Silence. No click, no cough, no engine even trying to sputter to life. He tried it again. And again. Then whipped his head around to glare at her shadow. "It won't run."

"No kidding?"

In spite of pain or panic, she had a sense of humor. A distinctly feminine sense of humor. It didn't endear her to him any. "Lady, you and I are in trouble up to our necks—and dammit, would you stop that?"

This time she didn't make a sound, but it was happening to her again. He could hear the rasp of her panicked breathing, see her shadow contort in pain. She rode it out pretty well, but Max bit his lip so hard he tasted blood. And then it was over again.

She said weakly, "You know...it's the first time in my life I ever wanted to be accosted by a drug pusher, and instead I get a farmer. I don't suppose you have any morphine in your truck? Morphine, heroin, cyanide, arsenic? I'm not picky—"

"Come on, cut it out. You're going to be fine. I have three sisters; they all had babies. Millions of women have babies."

She shook her head. "Not like this. It's all wrong. It's too early; the contractions are nothing like the doctor told me they'd be. I'm going to die—"

"Would you quit talking like that? You are *not* going to die," Max snapped, and jerked out of the car. "Now you just calm down and stay cool. I'll be right back."

She said something, but he didn't hear it, or want to. Maybe there was time to get her to a hospital, but he couldn't bank money on it—not at the rate those contractions were coming. He had no choice but to prepare, which in its own way was a relief. Max was far more comfortable with action than emotion.

He found two flares in the glove compartment of his truck. He lit both, set one behind her car and the other at the crest of the hill. Once that was done, he jogged back to raid the truck for supplies. He wanted boiling water, sterile scissors and string. He found a dusty yank of twine, his Swiss army knife and a glass of warm iced tea on the dash.

He carted that pitiful cache to her front seat, then yanked the key out of the ignition. "You doing okay?" he asked her gruffly, but he could hear from the uneven catch of her breath that she wasn't. She also wasn't in the mood to chitchat with a stranger. Hell, neither was he.

Wasting no time, he took the key around to the back. Unfortunately, her trunk was the same spotless wasteland as the inside of her car. All he found was a spare tire and an expensive, cowhide leather suitcase. The case would have frustrated a bank robber. It wasn't locked, but he had to grope with a half dozen fancy latches and belts before he could yank it open.

Once he did, more of that elusive, classy perfume assailed his nostrils. Some women smelled as forbidden—and dangerous—as sin. Whatever her name was—Kitt?—she was one of them. Irritated that the scent had distracted him, he pawed through the case. The only thing in it was clothes—silky stuff, satiny stuff, luxurious fluff that could arouse a monk's hormones . . . but nothing of any practical use. He toted a bundle back to the front seat anyway, then opened the back door where her head was.

She was in the middle of another contraction. So was he—at least his stomach felt as if a spiked mace were churning inside it when he saw her face screwed up in pain.

He had no time to sit around—God knew how fast the baby was coming—yet his heartbeat abruptly slowed and the adrenaline stopped pumping. With the door open, her face was moonlit.

He hadn't noticed before what she looked like. He didn't care. It didn't matter. And he still didn't care; it still didn't matter. But until that moment she'd been nothing more than a shadow in the back seat, grief he sure as hell didn't need, a problem.

She suddenly became real.

Everything about her was small. A bit of a nose, wispily arched brows and thick soft eyelashes whispering over elegant cheekbones. Her mouth had a smudge of color but only because she'd bitten her lips raw. Her hair was a silvery, ashy blond, and she wore it in a cut shorter than a man's. He hated short hair on a woman, but on her the style showed off her long white throat, delicate collarbones, the shell curl of her ears. She was female from the inside out.

She was also scared out of her mind, and Max didn't need to know her to understand that fear—real fear—was new to her. She wasn't spring young. The tiniest network of lines fanned around her eyes. Maybe early thirties? He could easily picture her swinging into a boardroom with that French-fancy haircut and bossy chin. She was used to control; it was in her eyes, and so were drive and determination—all those handy little ingredients so critical to achieving success on civilized terms.

Those kinds of strengths weren't worth diddly-squat when it came down to something as elemental as having a baby.

Abruptly he dug in his back pocket for a handkerchief. Hunkering down on the side of the road, he splashed some tepid iced tea on it. Clumsily, as best he could, he mopped her face and brow.

"Don't!"

Another time he might have smiled. She snapped
out that "don't" real bossy, but her chin tilted hun-
grily for the feel of the cool damp cloth. "Maybe you
could try not looking at me like you wanted to level an
ax on my head?"

She closed her eyes. "Don't take it personally. I'd
more or less feel that way about any male human being
on the planet right now."

"Yeah? I'm not too hot on the female of the species myself. A pretty odd bond to find in common for
two strangers in the night. Maybe we might even get
along."

Her lips curled—he almost had a smile, but it didn't
hold. She swallowed, and her small slim hand suddenly closed on his wrist. "You're not going for help."
She didn't make it a question. There was the defeat of
acceptance in her eyes.

"No. Maybe you still have plenty of time, but neither of us have a guarantee of that. Hopefully the
flares will draw the attention of a passing car, but it
doesn't much matter. I'm not leaving you alone." He
wrung out the handkerchief and dipped more tea on
it. His matter-of-fact voice seemed to calm her, but he
tried to give her a little more time to get used to the
idea that it was just him and her.

He brushed the cloth on her face again, trying to
soothe away the tears and cool her. He was afraid to
touch her directly. Her skin was impossibly soft, and
his big hands were all rough knuckles and calluses.
"So...where's Mr. Kitt?"

"There isn't one." Again, she briefly closed her
eyes. "It also isn't really my baby. I was supposed to
sign the adoption papers this Thursday. I thought

there would be plenty of time before the birth. It was all arranged."

"You don't want it?"

Bitterness laced her voice. "I lost my job, my career, in a way my whole life, because of this pregnancy. Thirty-nine-year-old women are supposed to be smarter than to get caught, right? And the funny part about it is that I thought it couldn't happen. Not to me. About a hundred years ago I was married for a short time. I ended up seeing a doctor—he diagnosed some fancy name, but it amounted to skinny tubes. The chances of my having a baby weren't zilch but close to it—and no, I can't keep it. Right now, I don't even have a job."

He noticed she said she couldn't keep it, which wasn't the same thing at all as not wanting it. "No family around?" he asked casually.

"Lots of family. All in Milwaukee."

"If you started out in Chicago, you sure took a wrong turn around the lake if you were headed toward Milwaukee."

"The last place I'd be headed is Milwaukee. My family's used to depending on me, not the other way around. My grandmother has a cottage on this side of the lake that no one's used in years. I've been moving things for the past few weeks, setting up there. This was supposed to be the last trip. The doctor, the hospital, the adoption—it was all organized."

Max would bet she was good at organizing things. He'd also bet that she rarely spilled so much private information in front of a stranger, but as they both knew, tonight was different. Talking for a few minutes had helped her block out what was happening, but he was well aware her wary dark gaze had been studying his face.

He could imagine how he sized up in her eyes. Next to her fragility, he was a wire-muscled brawler. He wrestled a living from the land, and his physical life-style showed from squint lines around his eyes to weathered skin to the grit under his fingernails. Next to her classy white elegance, he was a hundred and ninety pounds of whiskers and work boots and tough hard living.

Max let her look her fill, guessing she wouldn't find much to like or relate to, but trust was something else. By some miracle her contractions had quit for the last few minutes. Good luck never lasted forever. She'd had about all the time either of them could afford to decide whether or not she trusted him. "Kitt?" He propped the damp handkerchief on the back of the seat. "I'm afraid you and I are going to have to get to be best friends pretty quick."

"I don't understand."

He said quietly. "If you let me do a few things, I can make you more comfortable. For starters, I know it's plenty hot, but you have to be miserable in those wet clothes—" She never gave him the chance to finish.

"No."

"At least the slacks. I'm not saying I'm an expert on this, but it sure seems to me that it would be tricky to have a baby with pants on."

"No."

"I got some stuff from your suitcase to put under you. It's not exactly bedding, but it'll be better than nothing and at least it's clean."

"No."

Max patiently scratched his chin. "I had kind of hoped you'd figured out I wasn't a mad rapist by now—not that kinky sex doesn't turn me on, mind you. Variety is the spice of life, but a woman about to deliver... honest to Pete, sweetheart, it's just not one of my personal fantasies." When she tried to interrupt, he firmly continued. "A dog could figure out you don't want a man—any man—anywhere near you right now. In your shoes, I'd feel the same way, but from the time I got here, it's been all you could do to move your head. You don't have the strength to do for yourself, and I think you know it."

"Max?" With her eyes closed, she suddenly licked dry lips, and her voice was whiskey low. "I'm sorry. Sorry you stopped. Sorry you're stuck with this. With me. I'm not used to needing people, having to ask anyone for help. It's hard."

He didn't know what to say to her, so he didn't say anything at all, just lifted his hand. She had to think about it, but then she matched her slim fingers to his. Pampered skin bonded to calluses. Both squeezed, then held on tight.

It was the most poignant moment Max had ever shared with a woman—so much so that he felt oddly, dangerously off balance, as if an emotional rug had been swept out from under him and life could never be the same again.

The silly rash of sentiment didn't last.

A minute hadn't passed before she wrenched her hand free. A screech erupted from her lips that would make a banshee run for cover. Her water broke at the same time a contraction seemed to scissor her in half.

Two

———

I hate you, Max Carlson!"

"So you keep saying. It's not may fault we've been here all night. You're the one with the pumpkin. Obviously you can't thread a pumpkin through a needle unless you push *damn* hard. Haven't you ever done any manual work in your entire life?"

"It hurts!"

"So it hurts."

"I'm exhausted!"

"Tough. So am I."

"I'm going to die, and you're being cruel and callous."

"I keep telling you you're *not* going to die. Nobody could go through this much hell and then die. And we were doing a lot better when you were screaming your lungs out."

"I was *trying* to be quiet."

"What the heck are you trying to be polite around me for? Yell for bloody hell. Who's to know but you and me?"

"Max . . . I'm afraid."

"Of what now?"

"I'm scared I'll . . . tear."

"So you tear. As soon as you have this kid, I'll zip you in the truck and cart you to the hospital so fast it'll make your head spin. They'll sew up any rips so tight you'll think you're a virgin again."

"Do you have to be so crude? Is no subject sacred with you?"

"I don't think you want to have this baby. I think on some deep, fancy, hocus-pocus unconscious level you're trying to keep it in so you don't have to give it up. I don't think you ever wanted to give it up."

"You're dead dead dead wrong."

"So you say. Come on. Grunt like a pig. That's what my sisters said they had to do."

"The day I grunt like a pig is the same day I fly. You know so much about having babies, buster, why don't you have this one? Has it possibly occurred to you that maybe I just can't take any more?"

"Sounds like b.s. to me. If you're strong enough to fight with me, you're plenty strong enough to push."

"Are you completely incapable of sympathy? Understanding? Compassion?"

"Yeah, and all the other holy emotions that women worship like the Holy Grail."

"Don't judge me by your ex-wife's rhetoric, Carlson. It's not my fault you married a creep."

"And it's not my fault you hooked up with a turkey like Grant. Next time try to have the good sense to fall for guts instead of charm."

"My boss was not a turkey."

"Well, he sure as hell wasn't a man. He cons his way into a one-time shot in the sack and you end up on the side of a road. Doesn't take a Ph.D. to figure out he shares a lot of the same characteristics as horse manure."

"That's not fair, and it wasn't that simple."

"Sure sounds simple to me."

"Max?"

"What now?"

"I hate this baby and I hate all men, and most of all, of all things on earth, I hate you."

"Are we back to that again? And dammit, don't *cry*. I'm not trying to hurt your feelings, you stupid woman, I'm trying to make you mad. Come on, Kitt. Somewhere in there you have a little adrenaline left. Bring it up. Use it. Sweetheart, don't you think I'd have this damn kid for you if I could?"

It was still pitch-dark, but daybreak was only an hour away. Two cars had passed in the night. Neither had even slowed down, much less stopped.

Kitt would long have given into exhaustion and despair if it hadn't been for the unreasonable, cynical, crude, insensitive rednecked farmer hunched near her feet. Her best satin slip was draped over her legs, preserving what little modesty she had left. It wasn't worth much because he regularly peeked.

She'd never been in a more vulnerable, humiliating position in her entire life, and Max was blithely slicing his clean white teeth into a peach.

She was near starvation and her throat was parched, but he wouldn't give her any. To be fair, he'd offered her a slice of peach a few hours before. She'd promptly thrown up all over his shirt. If she were now dehydrated to the point of being comatose, he wasn't likely to offer her any more peaches.

The batteries in his flashlight were starting to fade. It didn't matter. By now Max's features were as familiar as her own.

He wasn't tall. He wasn't big. He had a thick head of undisciplined, unruly dark hair with a hint of steel in the sideburns; his eyes had the black snap of ebony and he was built like wire. Originally he was wearing a shirt and jeans. Now he was just wearing the jeans—they were filthy—and his sun-bronzed chest was a rug of springy dark hair. Kitt had always hated excessive hair in a man. It reminded her of gorillas and cavemen.

Max was neither of those, but he was a definite primitive force in the darkness. He had more restless energy than a cat. He never stopped moving. In looks, he was far more striking than handsome. His face was all hard planes—lean cheeks, square jaw, uncompromising brow and a crooked nose. His deep-set eyes were dark and bright, twin black fires in the flashlight's beam. His right eyetooth wasn't quite straight. He had a scar on his left shoulder. His jeans were so old and faded and shrunk from a thousand washings that they clung to his lean hips and hugged the private space across his zipper. Max flaunted the man he was. He was earthy, natural and primitively physical.

And Kitt had no doubt she'd have died without him. She had started out the day as a mature thirty-nine-year-old and an experienced marketing analyst—albeit a pregnant one—but she'd lost that entire civilized veneer hours ago. Never mind how unalike she and Max were. He was, and had been, absolutely the only thing she had to hold on to.

The contractions had yet to stop, the pain yet to ease. He was there. When she was screaming scared, he was teasing her. When she was trying to give up, he was goading her, arguing with her, distracting her. There had been a gushing mess when her water broke...it was nothing she could help, but with any other man—and especially a stranger—she would have felt intense humiliation and vulnerability. She felt that with Max, too, but he had no patience for modesty or manners, and maybe, just maybe, she'd stayed alive this long because he hadn't given her any other choice.

Nobody would mess with Max. Not if they had a choice.

Another contraction began, gripping hard, slicing. She knew it would get worse. How many hours had it been? A million. In her heart of hearts, the terror had long reached the unbearable point—the baby was going to die, or possibly already had. It was her fault. Because she didn't want it.

"Bear down, honey. Come on, Kitt. Come on, babe—"

Sweat poured from her brow. Her hands were gripped into fists. The darkness spun in starpoints under her eyelids. The splintering sharpness was relentless this time...yet oddly different. A strange, alien feeling of excitement mixed with the peak of pain.

The force of the contraction left her gasping. Max loomed over her, mopping her face with his handkerchief. She would associate the night for the rest of her life with the smell of stale iced tea and peaches and the look of Max. His eyes were fierce with fear and the worry he had yet to express. The gaunt planes of his face were intimidating in the shadows, yet his calloused thumbs brushed her cheeks with incomparable gentleness.

"A few more minutes and it's going to be over," he promised her.

"You promised that two hours ago."

"Yeah? But that was when I thought you were a city wimp. You're pretty tough for a duchess."

The compliment would have made her smile if she'd had the strength. She already knew how Max felt about "duchesses." They had each shared secrets in the darkness; there had been no other way to pass the hours and handle the anxiety that occasionally overwhelmed them both. Kitt knew he'd married a duchess named Andrea—also that Andrea had walked out on him four years before.

Max had married Andrea when he was twenty-four, relatively fresh from college and determined to make it in a desk job. His father's heart attack had forced him back to the nearly bankrupt family farm. When his dad died, Max could have sold out and left. Instead he'd stayed, driven by needs that wouldn't let him go. Fluorescent lights couldn't compete with the sun. Shuffling papers couldn't hold a man who needed the wind in his face and the physical challenges that went into being a grower.

His Andrea couldn't handle the endless threat of financial risks. Kitt understood how his ex-wife felt. A woman had a need for security—and that certainly included financial security—which wasn't possible in an up-and-down living like farming. The same challenges that drew Max had frightened his ex-wife…only that wasn't the way he saw it. Max only saw that his ex-wife had rejected him, who he was, all he was, all he knew how to be as a man.

Kitt could imagine what Max had thought when he'd first laid eyes on her—the car, her clothes, her, all of it. Another pampered suburban duchess.

And he was right.

But she wasn't much of a pampered duchess now. And Max must have seen something in her eyes, because he dropped the handkerchief and scuttled back down to hunker in his spot on the side of the road. Another contraction overrode the last one, then another, spaced not at all. She couldn't catch her breath, yet the instinct to push was suddenly stronger than pain.

"Come on, love. I can see the head. *Would* you get your hands off the stupid slip! How many times do I have to tell you, there's no one to see you but me?"

She forgot about Max. She forgot about everything. A contraction took her with the searing heat of fire, the cutting power of ice—Max roared something about seeing the shoulders—and then she nearly blacked out with the wonder of release.

Afterbirth cramps continued, but then they were done, too. For a few seconds she lay panting, eyes closed, her eyelashes sticky and matted with exhausted tears…but her heart stopped altogether when she heard another faint, weak cry.

"Max?"

"It's okay, it's okay. It's a girl! And she's fine."

"Are you sure?"

"Positive. Of course, she's a little messy right now...."

"Could I see her?"

"Just hold your horses for two seconds, princess. I kind of have my hands full down at this end. I clamped the cord but I didn't cut it, and she needs some cleaning up, but that's a little tough to do when all I've got to work with is blouses and nightgowns. Afraid you're going to need a whole new wardrobe after this little activity tonight."

"I want—*need*—my daughter, Max."

He stopped talking. She never saw him reach in. All she felt was the soft, light weight of the baby he laid on her breasts. A shadowy pearl sunrise was just starting to light up the sky. She could barely make out the soft fuzz of blond hair, the scrunched red face, one tiny squeezed fist no bigger than her thumb. Like a fool—it seemed she'd been nothing but a fool this whole night—she burst into tears. And held on, so carefully, so possessively, to the precious bundle of life she'd been so terrified of losing.

She had the crown of the baby's head nestled under her cheek when she looked up. Max's eyes were as exhausted as her own, but his gaze held hers in a rich, savoring bond. "You did it, honey."

"We did," she whispered. "Thank you."

"Yeah, well, we're not done yet. Let's hope she's a scrapper like you are, because her first experience in life is going to be a bumpy ride in a dusty ten-wheeler. I need a minute to get the seat cleared off in the truck and to set up some bedding. You going to be okay?"

"Fine."

"Kitt?"

Again she looked up. Again she found his eyes focused with relentless intensity on her and the baby.

"You're dreaming, sweetheart," he said quietly, "you are out of your mind dreaming if you think you're giving that tyke up for adoption."

The hospital was tucked in a valley on the St. Joseph River. Robins and orioles pranced between trees. The landscaped grounds were a wash of gold under the early-morning sun. It was a setting of utmost peace and serenity—or it would have been if there hadn't been a cop's siren screaming behind them.

Max's aging diesel truck hadn't seen seventy miles an hour in years, much less while hauling two hundred bushels of peaches. The emergency room entrance was located in a semicircular cul-de-sac. When he braked to a stop, the truck spit, sputtered and died.

Still bare chested—it wasn't as if he had a choice of wardrobe—he pelted out the door at the same time the cop in a tan uniform was climbing out of his car. "Hey," the cop said. "We're talking fifteen miles over the speed limit, running a red, and if you think you're going to park here—"

Max heard him. He just didn't pay him any attention.

He jogged around the front of the truck to reach Kitt's side. There had been a clinic closer, but only by a few miles, and this was where she'd set up the doctor—and the stupid adoption.

The ride had been hard on her and he knew it. There was no space for her to lie down, yet she was obviously too uncomfortable to sit, and his driving hell-bent for leather was no way for her to get any rest. She'd been through hell, and the baby was terrifyingly small—in fact, Max had never seen any human alive that small. He thought he'd been scared before it was born, but hearing that tiny thing screech at the top of its lungs... *that* was terror.

Still, when he reached in for Kitt, he couldn't help a wayward grin. The temperature had dropped at dawn. When she'd gotten cold, he'd wrapped her in his dusty denim jacket. The jacket was paired with her white silk blouse, bare feet and a powder blue satin robe he'd wrapped around her legs for modesty. He figured the duchess would call it quite a fashion ensemble. In contrast, the cargo on her shoulder couldn't be more classily attired. The baby's diaper was an imported Italian scarf, and she was swaddled in a Calvin Klein blouse with pearl buttons.

"How's our Jennifer Lise?" he whispered.

"Don't talk so loud, Max. She'll wake up again, and you don't have to do this. Don't you think they'll bring a stretcher?"

"And have you wait out here?" He saw her bite her lip when he lifted her, but she didn't complain. Maybe he should have gone in first and asked for a stretcher, but then she would have been alone. It bothered him enough that she was going to be alone in the hospital. No husband was one thing, but no family or nearby friends was another.

She didn't weigh much, but he wasn't built like Superman, either. He figured his back was going to be out for a week as he angled through the emergency room entrance. Kitt was too beat to hold up her head. Feathery strands of ash-blond hair tickled his chin.

"I've caused you no end of trouble," she said weakly.

"Don't sweat it."

"But your peaches, Max. Are they going to be okay?"

"Sure." He knew better, but there was no reason for her to know. She'd been through enough.

The action was fast after that. As he might have expected, Kitt had researched the most prominent ob-gyn man in town. One mention of the doctor's name and the hospital staff flew. Kitt was taken from him and rushed off before he could say anything else to her—and that was what should happen, exactly what he wanted to happen—but he still felt a moment's disorientation when Kitt and the baby disappeared behind closed elevator doors.

It couldn't be over just like that. The little shrimp with the fuzz of blond hair and the lungs like a coyote… That was *his* baby they'd just taken away. He'd held her first. He'd sworn and prayed and sweated her into life; he'd cleaned her off, counted her toes.

And Kitt. *No.* It wasn't as if they were anything to each other. A duchess in a chariot driven by a white steed and a farmer carrying half his topsoil in his boots weren't likely to meet again. But this was the woman who had shrieked at him when he'd pulled off her underpants. He'd dried tear after tear on those elegant high cheeks; he'd held her head when she'd thrown up all over his shirt; she'd damn near broken the bones in his hand during one of those contractions. They'd had a *baby* together. A man couldn't walk off and forget something like that as if it never happened.

Besides, he still didn't have a guarantee she was going to be all right. He also didn't know what she was going to do about the baby. Didn't that justify his sticking around a little longer?

God, he was tired. His eyes were burning and his stomach was growling empty when he saw the cop ambling toward him.

"I saw what was going on. Looks like you've had one heck of a night. We'll skip the tickets, but you still have to move your truck."

Max nodded. "Will do, and thanks." He added wearily, "There's a problem with her car. She's got a white Le Sabre, about ten miles off the interstate on a gravel road called Lake View. It needs a tow and a fix before it'll run. I'll call for the tow, but in the meantime it's a traffic hazard."

The cop promised to take care of it, and Max left to move his ten-wheeler. After that he found a phone to call the farm, a bathroom to wash off the first layer of grime and a coffee machine. All that took time, but not enough for him to locate Kitt. Apparently she had yet to be delivered to a bed on the maternity floor. That he wasn't direct family didn't help his inquiries. A lot of people seemed to think it wasn't his business.

If he couldn't find Kitt, he was determined to find out how the tyke was doing. The glass-windowed nursery was on the fourth floor, and the whole scene was a little bewildering. The urchins didn't look like babies. They looked like dolls—miniature dolls in miniature cribs—all wrapped up in white like Indian papooses.

There had to be at least fifteen or sixteen, and at first he couldn't spot her. They all looked alike, red-faced, swaddled and mostly hairless. From his viewing angle, he couldn't spot any fluff of blond hair, but the one in the sixth crib was squalling. He couldn't hear the squall through the soundproof walls, but the tiny puckered mouth was familiar.

He looked up with a scowl. The two nurses inside were racing around and doing nothing important—at least on his priority scale. When he pushed the door and stuck his head in, one of the nurses whirled on him. "Sir, you can't come in here."

"She's crying."

"I beg your pardon?"

"The one in the sixth bunk. She's crying."

"We know that, sir—" The nurse's hand extended politely toward him as if she planned to shove him out the door, but then she hesitated. "You have to be the one who came in off the highway this morning?"

News must travel fast in a hospital. Either that or his bare chest, whiskered chin and the half-moon shadows dragging under his eyes gave him away. "She's had a doctor check her out? She's okay?"

"She's just fine. An ounce under six pounds; her APGAR was a nine—it's hard to get better than that— and she's taken a little nourishment and been all cleaned up."

"She's absolutely fine? You're positive?"

"No question—"

"Then why is she crying? Why aren't you picking her up? Can't you do something?"

The nurses exchanged glances. Within ten minutes he was capped, gowned, bootied, gloved and masked. They gave him the nursery rocker, which had no arms, and maybe he felt a little foolish...but not too much.

The baby felt pretty good, considering that at the advanced age of forty, Max had long given up hope of holding his own child. Once he'd decided that arsenic was preferable to marriage, he'd accepted family life wasn't in his cards. If he had regrets, he rarely thought about them anymore. He also wasn't thinking about them now.

He set up a rocking rhythm more suited to rock and roll than lullabies—Jennifer Lise wasn't going to quit crying for any of that sappy stuff—and made gruff, low conversation to let her know who he was. Max. The guy with the rough whiskers who she'd met on a roadside in the back seat of a car. He told her she'd better not meet any other guys in the back seat of a car or he'd have her hide. He also told her that "Lise" was his mother's name, that Kitt had sleepily pounced on "Jennifer Lise" when they were tooling down the highway, and that any mother who picked out a name while she was gulping back tears was hardly going to give her baby up. She'd damn well better not.

Jennifer Lise listened to the entire conversation and then, her mouth making an exquisite little bow, yawned in heartless boredom.

Max fell in love.

Eventually the nurses figured they'd broken enough rules and threw him out, although they were kind enough to donate an orderly's coat so he didn't have to continue going around half-naked. Then, because he was going to keel over if he didn't, he sampled some breakfast in the hospital cafeteria. Still, it was early afternoon before he could see Kitt. Once she was installed in a room, either she'd fallen asleep or the head nurse was determined that she was going to. Either way, the dragon manning the maternity wing had closed the door on her room and wasn't letting any nonhusbands near it.

He kept telling himself he had a farm to run, a labor crew waiting for him, peaches spoiling on his truck—yet still he stayed. He just couldn't leave without at least saying goodbye to her. Eventually it wasn't the dragon lady who made it possible but Kitt herself, who apparently had wakened and was asking to see her baby. Since Max had installed himself as a permanent fixture near the nursery by then, he heard the order, and no one had any big problem with his wheeling the baby cart down to Kitt's room.

The moment he opened the door, he felt... awkward.

One look and he could see that she wasn't panicked now, she wasn't scared, she wasn't lost and tired and alone. There were still dark smudges under her eyes, but the few hours' rest had obviously refreshed her. Through thick and thin, she'd kept on her gold chain and earrings. On anyone else the jewelry would have looked silly dressing up a standard hospital gown. On her it was natural. She would have looked classy anywhere. Her ash-blond hair had been vigorously brushed and swept cleanly away from her face, accenting her patrician profile and elegant bones.

Her quick blue eyes zipped to his the moment he walked in. Her smile was immediate, welcoming and warm, but he couldn't lose the feeling of awkwardness. She didn't need him now. He didn't belong.

"Max! I called to you from the elevator but they wouldn't stop. I never meant for you to wait—I knew you had your farm to take care of—but I felt terrible at the thought of never having the chance to thank you."

He wheeled the baby cart next to her, which for that moment, at least, gave him something to do with his hands. Her voice was like whiskey—not cheap-whiskey rough but good-whiskey smooth—and it grazed his senses in a way that made him uncomfortable. "I couldn't leave without being sure you were okay."

"Thanks to you I'm fine." Her eyes crinkled with humor. "A little sore. And a lot embarrassed at everything I heaped on your head."

"Cut it out, okay? I didn't come up here to hear that stuff."

But suddenly, he wasn't sure why he'd come up here at all. The minute she saw Jennifer Lise, Kitt leaned over and lifted the baby from the crib. Her hold on the little one was soft and secure and possessive. Max saw the way she touched the baby, and he saw the sudden quiet sheen of moisture in her eyes. The atmosphere between them was two against the world. That was the way it was supposed to be.

God knew why he'd spent four hours worrying that she wouldn't realize what really mattered to her.

"I get the feeling you're not going to sign those adoption papers?" he said quietly.

Again her face lifted to his. "No."

"A snap decision?"

"I can't deny that," she admitted honestly. "I also don't know how on earth we're going to make it financially. All I know is that last night changed things for me. Making one mistake shouldn't be compounded by making two. I wouldn't blame you for not believing it, but I'm not a stupid woman, Max.''

''I never thought you were.''

''No?'' Again her lips curled, and her eyes shimmered in shared humor for all the grief she'd given him.

He smiled back but didn't mean it. He thought of all the endearments he'd called her—honey and sweetheart and love. He'd called her a few swear words, too. None of them applied now. She had her baby, the night was over, and they were, after all, no more than strangers or ever likely to be.

''You gonna be okay?'' he asked swiftly.

''Absolutely fine.'' She motioned to his denim jacket, which an aide had tossed in the visitor's chair. ''I was afraid I wouldn't get the chance to give that back to you.''

He picked it up without putting it on. Nothing was going to help his appearance by now. With his borrowed orderly's jacket, his work boots, grease-stained jeans and a nightful of whiskers, he could guess what he looked like in her eyes. And she looked like classy china with her porcelain skin and gold jewelry and soft pampered hands.

''Okay. You take care now,'' he said briskly.

''Max—''

But he was gone, out the door and walking fast down the corridor. What was there to stay for? Nothing. What was there to say? Even less.

He had his hands full with his own life.

And he sure as hell had never belonged in hers.

Three

—

Okay, okay, okay. Just take it easy. You've made it more than clear that you're in no mood for a walk on the beach.''

Kitt quickly brushed her sandy feet on the mat and turned the knob on the cottage door. Once inside, she hurriedly pushed at the straps of the front pack but not fast enough to suit her six-week-old daughter. When Jennifer Lise was unhappy, she liked everyone to know.

"Now there's no need to shatter glass. We'll go through our whole list, okay? First we'll see if you're hungry." Hefting the little one to her shoulder, Kitt made a beeline for the refrigerator. The day's formula was mixed, but heating it and putting the nipple on the bottle while holding a squalling infant took effort.

"You realize how much easier this would have been if you'd liked *my* milk? But no, you had to go for the fake stuff. Honestly, love, you do tend to do everything the hard way. Never mind, shall we give this a try?" She cradled the baby's head and aimed the nipple. Lise took a suck—one—then screwed up her face and spit out both nipple and milk at the same time.

"Okay. So hunger isn't the problem," Kitt said patiently. "Maybe we have a burp?" She rubbed the baby's back, which produced exactly nothing but another furious wail. She aimed for the stereo. "Okay. How about if we try a little soothing, calming Tchaikovsky?"

A concerto in D Major began.

The baby shrieked.

Kitt switched it off. "Mozart? Aerobics? Maybe you'd rather be wearing pink instead of white? What do you say we check for a wet diaper?"

Kneeling down, she laid the baby on a blanket and stripped off the disposable. Jennifer Lise immediately quieted. The diaper wasn't wet. Her daughter simply liked being naked. She chortled when Kitt leaned over and made a burble on her tummy, and then ruthlessly kicked her mother in the chin.

"Hey, you." Kitt chuckled. For a few minutes there was peace. While it lasted—and she knew it wouldn't—she sprawled in absolute exhaustion next to her naked daughter.

Late-August sunlight poured through the windows, landing on the hodgepodge of belongings that were partly Kitt's grandmother's and partly her own. The cottage wasn't big—just one long room downstairs that was both the kitchen and living area, with a bedroom loft up—but it was a humorous blend of objets d'art and sandy floors.

Gran's taste had run toward plastic plants, beat-up furniture, rock and roll and refrigerator doodads. Kitt had stored most of the furniture from her Chicago apartment, but brought with her the things she valued : her collections of jade and crystal, the stereo and her classical tapes, the original oil paintings, the two panes of three-dimensional stained glass. Next to the faded chintz curtains, the stained glass looked ridiculous. Her expensive jade carvings looked almost as silly as her gran's collection of fishing poles.

A kind decorator might call the style eclectic. Kitt called it temporary, and until this past week she hadn't worried much about it. Recovering from birth wasn't an overnight process, and learning to be a mom for the first time at thirty-nine was just as time-consuming. There was just her and Lise, and the bond with her daughter had been her whole world. Worry—once the mainstay of her life—had been banished off the map.

But Kitt knew it couldn't be that way forever. This past week she'd been thinking. Hard.

She turned her head and lovingly viewed her daughter's enthusiastic attempts to swallow her entire small fist. "I don't suppose there's any chance I could coax you into a nap?"

Oh, God. That dreaded word. Lise immediately turned red; her itsy-bitsy brow puckered like a storm cloud and the tiny mouth opened wide. Kitt hurriedly scooped her up.

"No, no, no. We don't want to do that again. Sweetheart, it's just not your day, is it? You don't want to eat, you don't want to sleep; and nothing I'm doing

seems to be right. Come on, we'll pace." The route
had been long established—around the chintz couch
to the window and view of Lake Michigan, past the
stained glass and crystal collection, around the scarred
pine table, past all the doodad magnets on Gran's
fridge and back again. Kitt patted, jostled, soothed,
crooned. Nothing worked. Not today. Eventually she
climbed the hardwood staircase up to the loft.

"I know what's on your mind—the same thing
that's been on my mind all week. You think we should
find him, don't you?"

Normally, the cedar-paneled loft was an idyllic
hideaway. Sun shimmered in from the skylight in the
slanted ceiling. Gran's old brass bedstead was
mounded with feather mattresses, and the smell of
herbs still lingered in the wardrobe. Kitt laid the baby
in the crib, plugged the rosebud mouth with a pacifier
and reached for a diaper. The baby spit out the pacifier and made her feelings about diapers more than
clear.

"You thought he was pretty special? And so did I,
but I already looked in the phone book. It's pretty
hard to track down a man when you don't know anything more than his name and that he's a farmer. Who
knows where he lives? And who says he'd ever want to
lay eyes on us again?"

Kitt fitted the baby's arm in a white sleeper with a
balloon print, cradled the little one in her arms and sat
in Gran's old scarred Federal rocker.

"I know I'm responsible for your future, love...and
I know you think I've made a pretty rotten job of my
life so far. It's not like we haven't discussed this before, but I wish you wouldn't judge me so harshly,

Lise. Sometimes people take a wrong turn. Sometimes people very stupidly value the wrong things, even when they're trying terribly hard to do everything right—and no, I'm not going to bring up my former lovers with you. The last time I tried to explain about Grant, you spit up all over me."

The baby seemed to be lulled by her soothing voice and soft rocking. Kitt, exhausted, leaned her head against the wooden rocker and made the mistake of briefly closing her eyes. Lise immediately let out a bellow.

"Okay. Sorry. I'll keep talking. Silly me, I thought you might like a little quiet for a change." Lise had heard her whole life history before, but Kitt crooned it out again. The context didn't matter; the baby only wanted the constant sound of her voice. But one-sided conversations, Kitt had discovered, could have some humorous repercussions. Justifying one's choices to a month-old infant could be an oddly humiliating experience.

When Kitt was eighteen, she'd known exactly what she wanted. Money, money, money. Lots of it. Hoards of it. Bank accounts stuffed with it.

The Lord knew, no one in her blue-collar family had shared that crass obsession. Whenever her dad was laid off, the car was repossessed. Sooner or later the electric company shut off the juice and the creditors started knocking. They'd lived hand to mouth, not because they'd had to but because the family philosophy was to spend it when you had it. Her mom lived on hope and her dad on wild promises...and Kitt had had an ulcer at thirteen.

The obvious means to security was money, and the obvious route to money was an education. Kitt had fought for jobs, good grades and scholarships, and midstream, when she'd married Sam, she'd fought and worked double jobs to pay for his education just as ruthlessly. Unfortunately, Sam had the same devilish charm and beguiling grin as her dad. He was quite happy having her do all the work. He was equally content gambling away her entire bank account, and what he didn't get then she'd had to spend to obtain the divorce.

At twenty-seven she'd found herself dead broke— again—but this time she was smarter. Marriage was no guarantee of security, and divorce was a sure route to poverty for a woman. Ergo, she set new rules for herself. No more marriages, no more getting taken in by charming scoundrels. What she had, she was going to guard and protect as fiercely as her heart.

"But I got lonely, Lise. You can't imagine how lonely. My job was exciting—I loved business—but ambition and challenges and even the good money weren't always enough. And you have to remember that I didn't know I could have you. Remember the skinny tubes the doctor diagnosed that I told you about? So I thought I was always going to be alone."

She'd never slept around but had definitely dated her share. All the men were intelligent, competent, successful overachievers—like her. She'd never had a relationship with a man that was less than...civilized.

Grant was her only unplanned encounter. For years she'd shared a mutual attraction with her boss that they'd both acknowledged, enjoyed and cheerfully done nothing about. They'd worked a hundred late nights together. They'd regularly shared a glass of wine when those nights were over. There was only one occasion when a few too many glasses of wine had turned into something else.

When, impossibly, she'd turned up pregnant, Grant had offered to pay for an abortion. Not only was she thirty-nine, but this was likely her one, rare chance to have a child—she wouldn't consider it. Weeks later, he'd offered to marry her. As he pragmatically pointed out, they valued the same things: money, ambition, success, drive. They were an unbeatable working team. They could draw up a prenuptial agreement to protect them both financially, and they could hire a nanny for the kid. Everything would work out.

Nothing had worked out. She'd turned down Grant's cold-blooded offer and spent the next few months watching her life go down the tubes. A fifty-five-hour high-pressure workweek was impossible with a normal pregnancy, and hers wasn't normal—she was sick as a dog. Her authority in the office deteriorated—it was something of a joke that she'd gotten "caught" at her age—and wining and dining clients in maternity clothes didn't cut the mustard. Kitt couldn't deny putting Grant in an uncomfortable position. She was the boss's "problem," yet job hunting in her particular field in her condition was a joke.

She'd quit at seven and a half months and set up the adoption. It seemed a bitter irony. She could not—would not—keep a child without a job to support them both. Yet she couldn't keep the job because she was pregnant. In the end, Grant hadn't forced her to leave. He'd just made it damned impossible for her to stay.

Kitt snuggled the baby's soft head close to her cheek, inhaling the scents of baby powder and baby and love. "You think I chose men who never gave a damn about me, don't you, Lise?" she whispered.

It had bothered her all these weeks...that she couldn't imagine Grant stopping for a stalled car. She couldn't imagine him holding her head or tolerating the embarrassing mess of labor or kneeling on the side of the road for a stretch of hours. Grant would have gotten help and considered that heroic. But to stick by her?

It wasn't just Grant but Sam, and every other man she'd been involved with. None of them would have stood by her. To criticize them was ludicrous, when those were the kinds of men she'd chosen to be with.

"Thirty-nine years old, Lise. Awfully late to discover that I've been looking in the wrong places for the wrong kind of man. And it's damn late to find out that there really is a different kind of man out there."

Still rocking, still whispering, she shifted the baby in her arms. Lise's eyelids were starting to droop.

"You think I should find him, don't you? But you're biased, darling. You want a daddy. All I ever wanted was someone I could count on, and I don't know what I'd say to Max even if I found him. Hi there? If you don't mind, I'd like to check you out. See, I had this nagging impression that you're the most special man I've ever met, and I'd like to find out if that's still true when I'm not screaming through a contraction and have all my clothes on."

Even the thought made her smile ruefully, and the baby's eyelids were fluttering, fluttering, fluttering.

Kitt possessively stroked the baby's cheek, and her smile died. A hundred times her good sense had told her to forget him. It should have been easy, yet nothing had been easy since her baby was born. Because of her daughter—*for* her daughter—her whole foundation of values had been tested.

And found wanting.

Her eyes closed on that painful truth. She really was of an age where she was running out of chances to make her life right. Finding the right answers was her problem. Max had nothing to do with that, yet she had tenacious memories lodged in her mind of how he'd been with Jennifer Lise, how he'd been with her.

Her whole life had been a barefoot race through the wrong dreams. Regrets? She had lots. But she was seriously afraid that no other regret would equal her not finding him again. The night she'd delivered Lise had been traumatic and clouded by overpowering emotions. Maybe Max wasn't half as special as she remembered.

But she had to know.

Max was on the forklift. He had one hand on the wheel, the other on the high-low controls and half a peanut-butter sandwich clamped between his teeth when the white Le Sabre drove in.

It was eight at night. His working crew had long gone home. The three-story red barn was older than the century and functioned as office, shop, packing line and storage space. It was as quiet now as the two pole buildings that housed the tractors and trailers. Two hundred acres of peaches stretched to the west, the orchards looking neat and pretty and catching the somnolent haze of the day's last sunlight. The big flat leaves of the aging catalpas lining the drive never rustled a branch. The farmyard was a dusty yellow, still and quiet.

The whole scene looked real peaceful, which, Max knew, was a crock.

He was behind. The last day of August was only midway through the peach season. At that time of year, a farmer was always behind. His spray rig had a broken nozzle. The limping Massey needed a diagnosis and repair before six o'clock tomorrow morning. Three more pallets had to be loaded and delivered to Litowski before midnight. He hadn't had time to mow his grass in three weeks, God knew when he'd last opened the bills, catching five minutes to fix himself a hot meal never seemed to happen, and yeah, he recognized her car.

He managed not to crash the pallet into the truck bed, but for that brief moment he forgot how to chew. A stale chunk of peanut butter tried to lodge itself in his throat.

Eventually he swallowed it, finished loading the last three pallets and switched off the forklift engine. The whole yard went silent, which was the first he knew his heart was hammering telling loud.

Kit had parked in the shade of the catalpa tree by the house and was still there. She'd spotted him, but then she hustled around the front of her car to open the passenger door. He made the not-too-difficult guess that she was trying to unhook a baby from a car seat, but it didn't sound like a baby. It sounded like a howling coyote.

He wanted to grin, and didn't.

All these weeks he'd worried about her. Alone, no job, no money, no preparations made for a baby she'd thought she was giving away. He'd throw her out of his mind. She'd sneak back in. He'd be nose to nose in a cussing match over price with his fruit broker, and she'd jump into his imagination, distracting him.

He'd finally decided to simply live with the worry, because seeing her was out of the question. Why he never wanted to run into her again had never been clear in his mind.

Now it was.

The way she was bent over the seat he had a fine view of her fanny. Her fanny wasn't exactly a new view. Six weeks before he'd had a far more intimate look at the same scenery, but it wasn't the same. On that dark sweaty night he'd been alternately praying and swearing as hard as he knew how, and no sexual thought had ever occurred to him.

It did now. The slender sloping hips and long, long legs were fully covered in white slacks. They weren't tight but they snuggled the shape of her elegant behind like a lover's cupped palm. She'd tucked in a breezy white blouse that made him think of female pirates—the sleeves were billowy and the pointed collar dipped low. A brass coin belt cinched her waist— the last time he'd seen her she hadn't had a waistline, although he could have sworn she'd had bigger breasts—and he caught the sunlit wink of crystal in her ears. Probably diamonds.

Since she was wearing sandals on bare feet, the lady undoubtedly thought of herself as dressed casual. Max scratched the whiskers on his chin and refrained from glancing down at his jeans and work boots. He knew

the jeans had a hole high on the thigh. The boots had
been through mud, sand and an irrigation blowout.
All in the last three hours.

Her hair was still shorter than his, still a sassy sweep
of ash blonde sculpted away from her face. He'd remembered her face as covered with dirt and tear
tracks; now there was no sign of either. Her skin was
flawless, except for a sunburned blush on the tilt of her
cheekbones. A little lip gloss made her fragile mouth
look sexy as hell, and no man in his right mind would
ever—could ever—forget those arresting blue eyes.

Kitt wasn't beautiful, but the issue was moot. She
looked exactly as he'd guessed she'd look by normal
light of day—as expensive as a bad mistake. His reaction should have been to break out in an allergic
rash. Instead, irritating him no end, his hormones
kicked in double time. He'd beat smoking, but the one
bad habit he'd never been able to shake was being attracted to the wrong kind of woman.

Why, lady? Why did you have to show up here?

"Max?" She was walking toward him with a ten-
tative smile . . . and ten pounds of caterwauling baby.
"I hope this wasn't the wrong thing to do. You're
probably busy."

"No, it's okay." Gnats settled in his stomach. What
was he supposed to do or say? Politely shaking hands
seemed a little ridiculous after what they'd been
through.

"I didn't know how to find you. Eventually I found
someone who knew you through the wholesale farmers' market, but even then . . ." She shook her head,
smiling again. Her smile was as contagious as the flu.
"I almost didn't do this. I told myself you probably

wanted to forget that whole night. I wouldn't blame you, but I also thought . . . possibly . . . that you might like to see Jennifer Lise. You kind of have a vested interest in what happened to her, and it kept bothering me that you might have worried."

"Yeah, I did," he admitted gruffly. He didn't mention that he'd worried a thousand times more about her than the little one.

His comment seemed to awkwardly end the conversation, but the evening sunlit yard was hardly quiet. In spite of Kitt's frantic patting and soothing, the urchin was revving up to a true siren's pitch. "She doesn't always cry like this. Usually she's an absolute angel—"

Max swiped his palms on the seat of his jeans and extended them. "If a little grime won't kill her, let's have a look."

The offer startled her. "Heavens, you don't want to hold her when she's crying."

"My sisters' kids spent the first six months of their lives exercising their lungs. A little crying doesn't scare me." Again he extended his hands and reached for the baby, taking care not to touch Kitt. Any physical contact might remind her of the intimacies they'd been forced to share together. Nothing embarrassed Max, but Kitt was a coin from a different mint.

Jennifer Lise let out one last caterwaul midair and then settled on his muscled forearm with a hiccup. Kitt had called her an angel. Max had his doubts.

This was no prizewinner. Wild tufts of blond hair spiked out from her head like a ten-pound punk rocker. Maybe her mother had no ballast, but the tyke had plenty. She also had the kick of a wrestler and the intelligence of a twerp—she made a tiny fist and promptly hit herself in the nose. The rosebud mouth opened to express another of life's injustices. Max touched her nose, and butter-soft blue eyes fluttered up to discover who was holding her.

She remembered him. Hell, no, he wasn't so stupid as to claim such an idiotic sentimental thing aloud, but . . . she remembered him. The blue-eyed focus was blurry, but she knew who'd pulled her out into spanking-bright life. So did he. It just didn't matter how many hard roads he'd traveled; a man couldn't forget something like that.

"Whatever you're doing, bottle it," Kitt whispered teasingly.

"Pardon?"

"She stopped crying."

"What happened to the tall tale about the angel?"

Kitt immediately defended her daughter. "She *is* an angel. For at least three minutes every day."

Max stifled a chuckle. "My sisters all had rebels, so I'm an old pro handling them when they're this size." He hesitated, aware that she was curiously and intently studying him—exactly what he was trying to avoid doing to her. "We don't have to stand out in the yard. I have some iced tea in the house."

"We can't stay. I don't want to be in your way. I know you're busy at this time of the year—"

"Don't sweat it. I've been on my feet since six this morning. A glass of iced tea would suit me, too."

"We can't stay," she repeated, but it was pretty clear the protest was token. She unloaded enough stuff from the car to visit in Europe for six months—first a purse, then a diaper bag, then a blanket, then a baby carrier.

Truthfully he knew from his sisters that the smaller the baby, the more paraphernalia it took for even a short sojourn from home. But it still looked as if Kitt were moving in, and the avid interest she showed when she ducked under his arm past the screen door made him real, real wary.

"What a wonderful home!"

"If you like inherited relics. Go ahead, look around. Spike and I can handle getting the iced tea."

She grinned at her daughter's less than classy nickname, but the whiskey softness in her voice had a trace of uncertainty. "Max...I really don't want to interrupt anything. Are you sure you don't mind?"

Max didn't know what he minded, but once Kitt was out of sight, he carted the pip-squeak to the freezer for ice cubes—about the only thing his freezer was filled with—and hauled the ice bucket to the counter. By a miracle he found two clean glasses and enough sun tea in the glass jug to pour. Blue eyes gravely watched everything he did. "Yeah, but you're gonna squall if I set you down, aren't you? And I'm stuck doing just that, because I have to wash my hands."

He whispered so Kitt wouldn't hear. He didn't want her to think he was one of those idiots who baby-talked to babies. The blanket didn't make much of a cushion on the hard counter but the baby didn't seem to mind. When he lathered his hands and forearms, she blew him a bubble.

"You and I could catch up on some old times, Spike, but I'll be damned if I know what to say to her. I never knew how to chitchat with women in the first

place. The last time I saw your mother, I had my
hands all over her in a place no man should have been
who didn't know her real well. That does *not* make
this visit easier.''

Another bubble.

''You're wasting your time. Charm, when found in
the female of the species, simply doesn't work with
me. You're gonna have to leave—just as soon as I find
out for sure if she's got enough money to eat on. I see
the pudge around your middle, but she's skinny as a
rail. Those fancy duds of hers won't pay the rent, and
I'm asking you straight. How broke is she?''

He dried his hands and scooped her up. ''Okay,
don't talk. I'll ask her myself. I'm all through staying
up nights worrying about her, Spike, but you have no
idea how short this visit is going to be.''

An hour later he felt the full power of a submarin-
ing blitz. She was still there. So was the tyke. And Kitt,
in mirthfully distracted fashion, had responded to all
his questions.

Max just didn't like a single one of her answers.

Four

So... what does your family think of the new addition?"

"Actually, they haven't had a chance to see her. My dad's been laid off so they're scrambling for a dollar right now. And I was afraid I couldn't handle the baby, not alone on that long drive around the lake, even if I'd had the cash to splurge on traveling ... this is wonderful, Max!"

Max clawed a hand through his hair. Kitt was bent over the living room fireplace, tracing the marble inscription that read For You the Firelight Gleams. The sappy romantic sentiment was not his cup of tea, and nothing he'd heard so far was "wonderful."

Her grandmother's cottage had been closed up for years. Kitt said she'd settled into it okay, but when he asked about close neighbors, she had none. The circle

of friends she'd made in Chicago were mostly business ties—naturally severed when she moved—so Max
had automatically assumed her family would come
through for her. They obviously hadn't, and he also
had the feeling they'd been sponging off Kitt for years.
No help from that quarter if she was broke. All these
weeks she'd been alone. Really alone.

Max cleared his throat. It had been aeons since he'd
exercised subtlety or tact. His voice was undoubtedly
rusty. "Of course, you probably had a little something put away. Even if you didn't originally plan on
keeping the baby, you knew you were stuck being out
of work for a short stretch."

"Hmm..." She squeezed his shoulder in a com-
forting gesture as she ambled past him toward the
stairway. "What kind of wood is this, Max?"

"Wild cherry. Your car running okay?"

"Fine, although I'm fairly sure I paid for the me-
chanic's new yacht by the time he repaired the ignition system." Inviting him to share the humor, she
shot him a grin—one of those dangerous, lethal, feminine grins that made him want to pat his shirt pocket
for an antacid. "I love the French doors, Max."

Swell. Max could have had a more rational conversation with a tree...or with the baby snoozing in the
corner of his couch. Kitt clearly wasn't herself. Possibly postpartum blues affected her powers of logic. It
certainly affected her sight.

No matter how fast he'd dashed around picking up
things, he couldn't make the place look like anything
but a pigsty. A wrench decorated his coffee table;
agriculture magazines cluttered the floor. So did socks.
He washed clothes when the supply of clean ones ran

out and applied the same principle to dishes. He hadn't dusted or vacuumed since the start of the farming season. No time. Usually he at least stocked his refrigerator, but he counted on rainy days to make a grocery raid. It hadn't rained in weeks. Occasionally a neighboring farm wife brought him a casserole—they understood what he was up against, trying to manage the farm alone, but Kitt couldn't and didn't.

He kept expecting her to be appalled at the debris, but there was no distracting her rapt attention from the house.

The family homestead was a giant two-story white elephant. The style was Dutch Colonial and had been built by his great-grandparents. They'd liked frills, starting with stuccoed walls and leaded glass windows and moving on to useless alcoves, an overabundance of fireplaces and an open wild-cherry-wood staircase more suited to *Gone with the Wind* than a farmer's life-style.

His great-grandmother had been a hopeless romantic. Max wasn't responsible. If it wasn't totally impractical for a farmer to live away from his land, he'd have camped in a hut and left the damn thing vacant.

"Brass chandeliers, fireplaces in every room, hardwood floors—no one builds like this anymore, Max!"

Thank God, he thought dryly. He nearly told her what it took to maintain a hardwood floor, then realized how easily she'd distracted him yet again. "So...any job prospects in the mill?"

"Zip," she admitted honestly. "Not that I expected there to be openings for a marketing analyst around here. I need a major city to do anything in my field."

"Then you're moving back to Chicago?"

For a moment her eyes looked liquid and lost, but not for long. She shook her head firmly. "If I have a choice I'm going to stay here. Doing what, heaven knows, but I'm not going back—not to smog and traffic and sixty-hour workweeks and a pressure-cooker job. That's no way to raise Jennifer Lise."

He agreed with her, but starvation was no way to raise Jennifer Lise, either. Kitt wanted and needed to make a career change. Nothing wrong with that, not if she was forced into it because of the kid, and she was already burdened with financial surprises that had hit her all at once. The whole situation confounded him. He was the one in threadbare jeans, she was the one in imported silk, so he was damned if he knew how to ask if she needed some cash.

She glanced at her watch and immediately flew for the baby, leaving a hint of Oscar de la Renta in her wake. The cologne smelled like sexual frustration. His hormones had been on a carbonated high ever since she walked in. Forty years old and he was as hard as a schoolboy. He chalked the problem up to a too-long period of abstinence but wished she would leave.

"I'm sorry, Max, I had no idea we'd stayed this long. If I don't get home, I'm going to run into Lise's night feeding, and you probably have a thousand things to do."

He did, none of which he could immediately remember. And maybe he'd just wanted her to leave, but now he was irritated that she was doing so. The shaming thought dragged his conscience that he'd been suspicious when she first drove in. He just couldn't imagine why Kitt had sought him out—unless she wanted something from him.

That cynicism was left over from his ex-wife—and a trio of sisters who never remembered his phone number unless they needed something—but Max should have known Kitt was different.

She had more pride than sense. It was in her eyes, in the aristocratic tilt to her chin, and he knew her. Even alone, on a black, bleak night on a deserted road, in trouble way over her head, she'd never expected him to stay. She'd expected him to make a phone call—and cut out on her.

She didn't think much of men.

That had bothered him, even knowing he shared a matching distrust of the opposite sex. It bothered him even more that she was now trying to split at the speed of light—without asking him for a single thing.

She had the baby, but that left a tide of paraphernalia. He picked up the receiving blanket, tangled the straps of her diaper bag and purse together and juggled the baby carrier under his arm while he tried to hold the back door open for her at the same time.

"I could have carried half of that," she protested.

"It's okay. You have your hands full with Spike."

Before, she'd smiled each time he'd used the nickname on Jennifer Lise—and maybe that was why he'd done it. She didn't *not* smile this time, but for the oddest moment she hesitated on his back porch.

The sun had long set, and the night was as black as a blackboard. Her face was lifted to his, and the yard light glowed on her pale skin. There was something in her eyes—a searching intensity, a shine of some fragile emotion. He didn't understand, and before he had the chance to, she turned away.

As quietly as he could, he stuffed the baby things in her back seat. As quietly as she could, she tried to stuff the sleeping Lise into the contortionist straps of the car seat without waking her. They both seemed to close the car doors and straighten at the same time.

Another awkward moment. For Max, her whole visit had been full of them. He hooked a thumb in a belt loop, for lack of anything better to do, and kept his other hand busy rubbing the tired muscles at the back of his neck. "She's something," he murmured.

Kitt didn't have his problem with nerves. "I notice you didn't try out any meaningless platitudes like 'what a beautiful baby she turned out to be.' "

His mouth twitched. "She's a scrapper. That's better than beautiful any day."

"She isn't a scrapper. She's a general, fully capable of commandeering every room in a house within minutes of arrival. You heard her set of lungs, and *that* was at eight in the evening. You should hear them at three in the morning sometime."

"A little transition for you from desks and marketing reports and clicking down a hall with a briefcase?"

"A little," Kitt said lightly. "Poor Lise—she's the one stuck with a mother who doesn't know anything. Some days I feel like I've been thrown out of a plane without a parachute; others, it's no worse than being caught in a hurricane. Even so, I seem to have become just a wee bit attached to her."

"You're sure? If you take her back, you could probably get a model with hair that doesn't take mousse to lay down."

She chuckled and took a step toward him. "She's the best thing that ever happened to me, Max. And that's really why I came here. To tell you that. To thank you. I had the feeling when you saw me that you weren't all that happy we showed up—I've made you uncomfortable and I'm sorry—but I honestly have to do this."

He saw her lift her arms. He couldn't have been more startled if she'd pointed a gun at his head.

He would have known what to do with a pointed gun. He had no idea what to do when her wrists hooked loosely on his shoulders.

All these weeks he'd built up the misbegotten image of Kitt as an untouchable duchess. Now he discovered there wasn't a moral in her, not an ounce of kindness, not a shred of honor—because she lifted herself up and, with the slightest tilt of her head, kissed him.

She shouldn't have, and if she'd had the sense she was born with, she wouldn't have. Her scent shot a bolt of heat through his bloodstream. The texture of her delicate mouth fanned the flame. Her car was a step away from the chaperon yard light. The darkness enveloped the two of them in their own private shadow, and oh, how she excited him.

She applied no pressure. The graze of her soft lips communicated nothing of seduction, nothing of teasing allure. The kiss was what she'd implied—a thank-you, for her daughter, for being there for her, for being someone she could count on one dark night.

She immediately pulled back, but not far. Her fingers were still tightened on his shoulders when her eyes met his. On a July day in 1980, Max had been stranded in an orchard when he'd seen a funneling cloud spiraling toward him. The memory was indelible in his mind—he knew the tornado was going to hit, but the reality wasn't half as bad as that gut-wrenching wait for danger.

He hadn't remembered that in years, but one look at Kitt's soft spike-lashed eyes, inches from his own, and he remembered it now.

She knew what she was doing. She wasn't a young girl kissing on blind impulse. She was a woman, with a woman's awareness and experience. Maybe the first kiss had been innocent, but she wanted a second. She'd come for a second. They'd formed an incomprehensible bond one long-ago night. She wanted to know what it was worth. She wanted to know if it was still there.

Only a heartless dog would take her up on the invitation in her eyes. Any bond they'd had was a creation of the circumstances. She couldn't last a day in his world. He had no tolerance for hers. Max was willing to label himself a bastard, but there was an honorable line even bastards didn't cross.

Yet there was no sound but the crickets, no light but the one in her eyes. She kept looking at him, waiting, wariness in her eyes but also curiosity and need. She wanted an answer, even if it took facing rejection.

Hell. His blunt hands slid in her hair to hold her, and his mouth clamped down hard in a different kind of kiss, one earthy and elemental.

There was no way he could reject Kitt...and no way he had to. He figured she was indulging in one of the more classic women's fantasies—the old one, about the ruthless cad kidnapping the virgin princess. Max knew the script. His ex-wife had turned on to the idea of muscles and physical strength. And hell, yes, he'd been turned on by the temptation to peel off the civilized layers and let the princess know what it was to be naked. Really naked. Soul-stripped naked in passion.

The fantasy had always sounded good to Andrea. For her, and him, it had always gone bad in reality. A lady who fastidiously bathed in lavender soap inevitably wrinkled her nose at the smell of a man's working sweat. And calluses had no real sex appeal.

Max had a day's grime on him, grease on his jeans, stubble on his chin and sweat sticking to his "big, manly" muscles. He figured Kitt wouldn't take long to get the message if he played it straight. So he played it real straight . . . only when his kiss roughened, deepened, she didn't pull away. She made a sweet yielding sound and clung.

Max had no idea when his eyes closed, but he knew damn well Kitt wasn't Andrea. His ex-wife had been smart like a fox. Kitt didn't have a brain in her head.

Her body swayed blindly to his. She fit him like a hot glove on a cold night. She drew him, like that crisp red apple had drawn Adam. And she shook him. Like he'd never been shook. Her nipples hardened into tiny buttons that he could feel. Her slim thighs braced against his, and when he ran his hands down her spine, he felt her small fanny tightening. She shuddered, hard. He'd never forgive her for that shudder.

She was no untried virgin. She had to feel the swell of his arousal against her abdomen. Still, her tongue met his. Still, her lips rubbed in lonesome response to his demanding pressure.

Her hair felt like a slide of silk under his hands. Softness. He couldn't remember when he had last felt it. Yearning. He hadn't allowed the emotion in his soul in years. And trust. Damn her, damn her. Max had been down too many hard roads to risk that kind of disillusionment again. Yet for a brief moment he could almost believe that a woman's promises meant something. At least her promises. Her wild, shivery response was too potent, too raw and vulnerable, to be less than honest.

So was his. His blood had always fired hot, but not like this. His heart was slamming, his pulse skidding. There was a baby not three feet away. And two hundred acres of farmland that were on the line this year surrounded him—he never forgot that, not for minutes, not for seconds. The land was the only thing he'd ever counted on. It was everything to him.

He abruptly jerked back from her, sharply aware that he was close to losing his mind because of her. Desire still thrummed through him, not sense, as his gaze focused hard on her shadowed face. Her breathing was uneven and her lips slightly parted. She looked nineteen, not thirty-nine. She looked . . . defenseless.

He'd known what to do when the disastrous tornado had hit. He had no idea what to do with her. With clumsy fingers he tried to push her hair back in place. He could fix her hair, but he couldn't fix the look in her eyes. "You have to go home," he said gruffly.

"Yes." But she didn't move. Her eyes closed suddenly, as if she were shaking herself awake, and then her lips tucked in a smile. "I give up. Did I just scare you, Max, or me?"

"You didn't scare anyone. You're beat. So am I. And hormones have a habit of slipping the gate when they've been tethered too long. Don't worry about it."

Her smile slipped, then stilled.

Kitt had had to whip on her best suit of courage to even come here. A woman didn't invite rejection unless the stakes were high. She'd needed to know if Max was the same man she remembered...and she'd found her answer. He'd nipped a slice of her soul, in the way he looked at Jennifer Lise. He'd moved her heart with all his less-than-subtle nosy questions. Max was fiercely protective, an honest, earthy, loving man. And a lonely one. When she'd wandered that wonderful old house with its bomb-squad clutter, the silence had hit her first. Too easily she could see Max rattling through all those empty rooms, alone, seasons passing.

But five minutes after she'd arrived, Kitt also knew she was going to let it go. Conversation was rough going. Max felt awkward around her, wary. He not only didn't relax, he didn't try. The rare, disturbing, special below-the-belt honesty she'd felt with him that night on the road—there was no way, none, Max wanted that door open again.

Only he'd opened it again with that embrace. The blood was still whispering through her veins, her heart still singing like a schoolgirl's.

But Kitt had never sung that rhythm and blues when she was a schoolgirl. Every rafter in her attic was still shook. At her advanced age she was more than a little unsettled to discover something missing in her birds-and-bees textbook. Passion wasn't new. Sex wasn't new. Finding a man who could shut out the whole damn world when he touched her—that was new.

She would have made love with him in a meadow. In a cave. In the ocean. In the desert. Anywhere, on any terms he wanted. Loneliness had poured out of Max, so had tenderness and need, and she'd responded from her heart.

His brusque "don't worry about it" cut like a blade. And his brushing off the emotion as "hormones" hurt even more. "Is that how you want to see it?" she asked him quietly. When he didn't answer, she lowered her head.

As if she suddenly noticed her hands were still on his shoulders, she dropped them. Just as quickly she spun on her heel and wound her way around the front of the car. "Good night, Max."

He wanted to kill her. She sounded that hurt. "Just hold your horses there, duchess."

She opened the car door. He thought for a minute she wasn't going to wait, but she hesitated, her eyes meeting his over the moonlit car roof. He figured he had about two seconds before she walked out of his life for good. It wasn't likely she'd give him more time than that. "You want a job?"

"I beg your pardon?"

He was sure she did. The words clearly came out of a man who'd lost his sanity. "A job," he repeated. "Work. Nothing big or fancy. I'm three weeks behind on bookkeeping and stuck with a weekly payroll of about forty men. It's nothing like your marketing field, but if you can run a calculator you can do it. Wouldn't take more than twenty hours a week. I don't care what hours you pick and you can bring the baby—Spike's no sweat—and at least it would keep you in grocery money until you're on your feet."

She took a long time to answer. "Did you think I came here for grocery money?"

He thought she'd come here to cause him more trouble than he could handle, and she had succeeded brilliantly. At that precise moment he didn't care. He would handle wanting her. Kitt was a measurable danger now. Take his old disastrous habit of being attracted to the Wrong Woman, accelerate the electricity about three thousand times, and there was Kitt. Bad trouble... but not if he kept his jeans zipped and his hands off her. That wasn't tough.

Worrying about her being jobless and broke—*that* was impossible. "I wouldn't have made the offer if I didn't need help. At this time of year I need six hands and I only have two. If you'd ever been around a farm you would know that's true."

Still she hesitated. He guessed she didn't want him to think she needed money. Either that or working for a farmer was beneath her. He was starting to feel defensive when she murmured, "Yes."

"Yes?"

"Yes, I'll take your offer, and thanks. When do you want me to start?"

"Whenever you want...except definitely sometime before Friday. The crew gets paid first thing Saturday morning, so I need to show you the ropes at least a day before that. The rest can work around your convenience.''

Those cool blue eyes studied him for a moment, immutably female and worrisome. He wanted to be able to read her and couldn't. He felt she was reading him instead—no one did that to Max and the sensation was irritating.

Her voice, by contrast, was soothing and light. "Sounds fine.''

A muted wail drifted from the inside of the car. Kitt ducked her head, then lifted it again with a smile full of fresh sparkle, but not for him. "Another country just woke up. Pray that we're not arrested for excessive noise before I make it home—and this time I really mean it. Good night, Max.''

The next day was Tuesday. Max left the house at six in the morning and didn't make it back until nearly five. His stomach was growling hunger and his throat was parched. Dinner would have to wait; he needed to flick on the weather-band radio. Clouds were rolling in from the west. He wanted a forecast of rain, but a storm with too much wind would put his peaches at risk.

He took the two porch steps at a clip, banged through the screen door and flipped on the weather band at the same time he reached for the cold tap and a glass. He was gulping a cool draught of well water before he realized anything was wrong.

"... a front moving in over Lake Michigan at approximately thirty miles an hour. The storm's expected to hit the northern shoreline at ...''

The glass in his hand was clean. It couldn't be. His sink smelled of bleach and disinfectant, another hallucination, and there wasn't a single dirty dish on the counter.

"Small craft advisories. This is a fast-moving front..."

His floor was shining. The last time he'd seen the redbrick tiles they'd been layered with dirt and boot tracks. Cupboard doors were closed—he never bothered—and a Dutch oven was sitting on his stove. He touched the lid, burned his hand, swore and fumbled around for a pot holder.

"...storm warnings..."

When he lifted the lid, the smell damn near unmanned him. Potatoes and carrots and beef bubbled in a savory stew. On the counter, an unfamiliar kitchen towel covered a loaf of fresh bread, still warm. A fruit salad of peaches and blueberries was plastic wrapped in his fridge. The pie was lemon meringue.

It was a hell of a thing to do to a man who'd been trying to live off snatched peanut-butter sandwiches for weeks.

"Repeat: storm warnings..."

There was no note, no sign of the brownie who'd done this to him. Max had been in and out of the barn office all day. Nobody had touched the bookkeeping—he still couldn't find the phone for the clutter of paperwork on the desk—so she hadn't been there. Bookkeeping was what he'd hired her for, and the mental image of Kitt washing his floor on her hands and knees in her whites and golds—no. It couldn't be her.

But what confounded Max was that it couldn't be anyone else.

Tuesday was disturbing enough, even if the threat of a storm never came to pass, but when he came in from the field on Wednesday he found his office sanitized, sterilized and spotless. She still hadn't gone near the book work, but he could see the floors. He could even see through the windows, and in the house he found his wash done. All of it. Even the socks. She'd starched his shirts, but he didn't realize that until Thursday.

Thursday, mid-morning, he was bent over a fitting for an irrigation sprinkler under the blazing sun. A trickle of sweat ran down the nape of his neck. It turned into gum. Sticky, itchy gum. Starch was real nice for a slick dude trying to look crisp in an office. It was plain uncomfortable for a man who made his living doing physical work.

The starch drove him nuts all day... which was beginning to be a familiar feeling. Not the starch. Going nuts. He didn't *want* her doing all this stuff, and if he'd caught her he would have stopped it.

He couldn't catch her. If she had a phone at the cottage, the listing was evidently under her grandmother's last name, because Information couldn't rouse it under hers. And as far as catching her on the farm, Max was sporadically in and out of the barnyard all day, but that wasn't good enough. Kitt was proving faster than a phantom and just as elusive.

Tomorrow, though, was Friday. Tomorrow she couldn't slip in and out without his knowing, because he had to teach her the payroll before she could do it. Tomorrow he'd catch up with her. Then he planned to find out exactly what the crazy blonde thought she was doing.

Five

Kitt parked in Max's driveway, retrieved the stroller from her car trunk and, quiet as a thief, transferred her napping daughter from car seat to stroller bed. Lise stirred but didn't waken—a miracle—and Kitt didn't dawdle steering toward the barn office. The farmyard was empty. That miracle wouldn't last long, either.

Every stereotype she'd ever assumed about farm life had been keelhauled in the past week. Farms were supposed to be pastoral and peaceful. Not Max's. If there wasn't a semi roaring in, there were tractors or forklifts or spray rigs kicking up dust. The phone rang off the hook. Some kind of machinery was always being fueled; some kind of equipment was always being hauled in the shop.

Kitt's preconceived image of farm workers was camera-ready Norman Rockwell. Bib overalls. Snapping suspenders. Ruddy faces. Strong backs.

Max's crew looked like refugees from a street gang. Some were Spanish, some not. They all wore long sleeves and dark clothes and hats that shaded their eyes, and Max's head honcho looked downright intimidating. She'd heard someone call him Moshe. Moshe wasn't Spanish. He was like a bear of the uncivilized, grizzly nature—big, bulky, black haired and bearded, and what little she'd seen of his face had been down a lot of hard roads.

Give or take the wad of tobacco in his cheek, Moshe was really very sweet—she'd talked to him twice. Kitt had few illusions that Max would be equally sweet when he caught up with her this afternoon—and that was inevitable, this was Friday—so she wasted no time wheeling Lise into the barn office and settling into the creaking desk chair.

It was the first chance she'd had to dive into the paperwork mountain. Max's absence hadn't inhibited her. Filth had. The office was tagged on the end of the huge red barn. Windows wrapped two sides of the structure. The inside floor space left you room to breathe only if you didn't have to exhale. Two filing cabinets, a crammed bookcase and a metal desk were all packed in the space.

Two days before there had been enough topsoil inside to plant a garden. She'd lost two nails and blistered her thumb cleaning it up. Max hadn't asked her. Very likely, Max wanted things just as they were.

Kitt kept waiting for her conscience to come up with a guilt attack. She was interfering in a man's life, a man who'd made it very clear he didn't want any woman—and maybe especially her—near him. Kitt had ethics, integrity, pride.

All of them had malfunctioned since last Monday. Lightning fast, her fingers sifted and organized the papers on the desk. She had no time to look out the windows, but the problem of Max was as complicated as the view.

The east window showed a rolling stretch of orchards. All those acres, all those orchards...yet there wasn't a single weed, not even on the roadsides. Every row was perfectly aligned, every tree looked babied, and the sod carpeting the orchards was picnic perfect.

In contrast, the southern window view framed his yard. The lawn was unkempt and the grass calf-high. The house was absolutely wonderful but, as Kitt knew, the inside was in worse shape than a rat's nest. Farmers, if anyone, should know enough to eat well. Max's cupboards were bare. Farmers traditionally went to bed with the sunset. As far as Kitt could tell from his unrumpled sheets, Max didn't go to bed at all. He crashed in a living room chair when he was finally too exhausted to keep going.

Maybe he wouldn't admit it, but Max needed help. Kitt was as equipped to provide that help as a duck out of water, a martian stranded on earth...a city slicker on a farm for the first time.

But dammit, there didn't seem to be anyone else.

And she owed him.

A man reaped what he sowed. Kitt refused to feel guilty for interfering when Max had asked for everything he got. First, he'd been stupid enough to stand by her that night on the road. Second, he looked at

Jennifer Lise as if her daughter were the sun and the moon. Third, he'd assumed she was the kind of witless, irresponsible jerk who'd allow herself to be dead broke—and even thinking her a turkey, he'd offered her help.

Kitt had carefully considered whether a certain lingering, disturbing, unsettling memory of an embrace had anything to do with her coming back. It didn't. It couldn't. Good grief, the idea of her chasing after any man in her condition was the stuff of comic strips—an unemployed, unwed mother with a tummy that still jiggled like jelly. And even before the pregnancy, a trace of sag and cellulite had started to show up. Kitt needed to risk the humiliation of getting naked with a man like she needed a bout of pneumonia.

She didn't want to get naked with Max.

She just wanted to help him.

A half hour later, Lise stuck her thumb in her mouth. Kitt's left hand automatically wrapped around the stroller handle and started rocking. Her right hand was still shifting papers faster than a machine.

Without specifics from Max she couldn't forge ahead with the payroll, but getting a handle on his accounting system was something else. Maybe she knew zip about farming, but this was her turf. An office was an office, a time card a time card. Accounts payable and receivable were universal business language, and a fifth grader could follow Max's ledger bookkeeping system.

"Shhh," she crooned to the baby, but facts and figures were swirling in her head like a fast-moving kaleidoscope. Good heavens. Three-quarters of a million bucks flowed through Max's hands in the course of a harvest season. He was also in hock right up to his seventeen-inch red neck.

A check for twenty thousand dollars floated free from a dog-eared file. The check was dated four days earlier. It could have been earning interest in a money market for those four days, but Max hadn't cashed it. How could a man have time to make a bank run if he couldn't even find time to open last months' phone bill?

Everything she saw affirmed what she already knew. Max needed either a keeper...or some serious, practical help. And fast.

A distracting roar and rattle made her glance up. The cavalry was zooming in from the orchards, led by a dusty tan pickup whose bed was overloaded with jostling, back-slapping workers. Just beyond were two tractor-driven trailers mounded with peaches.

She barely had time to leap to her feet before Max braked in the shade of a catalpa. His head swiveled to her La Sabre, then instantly to the open office door. He spotted her.

A forklift roared to life; bodies disappeared into the shop; pallets appeared from nowhere. Max directed the frenzy of activity, but his forefinger continued to waggle in her direction. *Stay. Right there. And don't you dare move, woman.*

Kitt was already braced for a little confrontation. Even so, she was briefly tempted to chew on a fingernail. When the last employee had been given instructions, Max strode toward her with a hip-rocking gait. His jeans looked as if they'd been rolled in dirt. His boots had been in a mire. He had to smell like hot sun, clean sweat, fresh earth and man...and the look of him went straight to her senses like a warm shot of whiskey.

For a spare second, her unconquerably cool smile faltered. The closer he came, the more she felt a slipping, a softness, a nagging whisper in her soul that she'd been lying to herself. He filled the doorway with about a hundred and ninety pounds of physical male power. Her pulse wasn't thumping because of any anticipated confrontation but because it was him.

There was no way he needed to know that. The moment Max opened his mouth, she raised a forefinger to her lips and motioned to the baby. That silenced him for a second. He cast a gentling glance at Jennifer Lise, but she wasn't so lucky.

His gaze skidded along the length of her, taking in her strappy sandals, salmon jumpsuit and gold drop earrings. He shook his head, wiped his forehead and shook his head again. "It's about time I caught up with you. You and I, Ms. Sanders, need to have a little talk."

If a man could growl in a whisper, he was doing it. "We certainly do," she agreed breezily. "I've gone about as far as I can until you give me the details on the payroll."

"I don't give a damn—" again he checked himself and lowered his voice "—about the payroll."

She nodded peaceably. "You're absolutely right. It's not the first priority, and I'm sorry, Max, I'd have put your bookkeeping on the front burner before this, but I didn't realize—"

"I don't give a damn about the bookkeeping, either. I want to know what the sam hill you think you've been doing playing housekeeper!"

The loose fists he hooked on his hips made him look saddle-tramp tough, and Kitt was beginning to enjoy herself. "Tough" might effectively intimidate his work crew, but she'd apprenticed in the business world. Corporate moguls didn't claw their way to the top on their sweet personalities. She'd bottle-fed men in a temper before.

"You don't like my lemon meringue pie?" she asked amiably.

"I'd kill for lemon meringue pie."

"You don't care for homemade bread?"

"I never said I didn't like homemade bread. Dammit, don't get tricky on me, Kitt."

"Tricky?"

"Don't be like a woman. Tricky. Evasive. Confusing."

"Ah," she murmured.

Max winced and ran a finger along the inside of his collar as if his neck itched him. It should. Red was skating up his throat as sure as a rash. "I'm sorry. I didn't mean that the way it sounded."

"No?"

"No. And you know what I meant." Impatiently he reached behind him to close the door. One of his workers was jogging toward the office. He didn't seem to realize it; he was too busy lowering his tone to a distinctly male version of calm and reasonable. "Honey, I didn't hire you to be a housekeeper. I hired you to do some bookkeeping. And if I'd wanted a housekeeper—which I don't—I would never have asked you to wash my floors."

Again, his gaze raked the length of her. The physical sparks between them could have jump started an ignition, but that, Kitt was sure, was not what Max was trying to communicate. She plucked at the collar of her jumpsuit.

"You wouldn't be trying to label me a spoiled, never-worked-a-day-in-her-life sissy because of my clothes, would you, Max? My previous life-style didn't exactly call for steel-toed work boots. Short of buying a whole new wardrobe, I'm stuck wearing what's already in my closet."

"You're doing it again," he said ominously.

"Doing what?"

"You're deliberately making this conversation confusing. Your clothes have nothing to do with this. I don't care whether you wear sackcloth or mink, I *don't* want you washing my socks."

"Trust me, Max. They needed washing. Either that or you'd have had a fumigating bill. Actually, I'm not quite sure why you're so upset over a little house-cleaning, unless..." She snapped her fingers and said with Sherlock Holmes shrewdness, "I get it! You're worried about my ulterior motive. Obviously I have the same chromosome as your ex-wife, and there's no possible reason a woman would volunteer to wash your socks, unless she had a sneaky, vile, loathsome hidden agenda."

Max scowled, but Kitt could see he had to work at it. The corner of his mouth started to twitch, and the starch was seeping out of his shoulders. "Fumigating, hmm?"

She delicately held her nose to illustrate.

He rubbed a hand over his face but couldn't quite hold in a chuckle. "You weren't half this sassy that night on the road."

"You weren't half as suspicious. I thought we'd gotten to know each other pretty well that night. Honestly, Carlson. I called you every dirty word I knew and screamed my head off just to please you. I thought we'd kind of mastered direct communication. Like if you want to know why I washed your floor, why the sweet petuties don't you just ask me?"

"Kitt?"

"What?" If he was going to grin at her like that, she was never going to get her blood pressure under control.

"Why the sweet petuties did you wash my floor?" he asked quietly.

Abruptly she sobered up. It wasn't easy to concentrate. Lise was starting to fuss; Moshe's face kept poking around the window, and a pair of men were hovering near the door. Max's world wasn't going to stop simply because she wanted to say something to him.

"I owe you," she said softly. "I owe you for my daughter's life, and maybe for mine. I'd given up when you showed up, Max, and that's just not something that I can forget. Our bookkeeping deal is fine, but that's an equal exchange, money for labor. I need to do something for you—"

"Honey, you *don't*."

She shook her head, determined to finish her piece. "I need to do this, and I have the time. In principle I should be spending my spare minutes scouring the want ads, but for the first time in my life I'm not sure where I'm going, what I want to do." She took a breath. "Lise screams like bloody murder if I put her in a playpen, but she's an angel when I carry her around in the front pack, so it's nothing for me to push a mop, throw in a load of clothes. I like baking bread, I love fussing with a meringue pie, and I haven't had the time to do either in a million years. Do you really have such a terrible problem with that?''

"Honey—"

"As far as I know, we haven't been in your way. We haven't even crossed paths. Have we bothered you at all so far?''

Max didn't immediately answer. He leaned back against the door and shoved his hands in his pockets, frowning. Their eyes met. His were worried, but warm. Kitt knew she'd reached him. He understood her need to pay off an emotional debt just as he understood her need for an oasis of time before job hunting. Max—the suspicious, woman-hating toughie—was incapable of turning down a woman who needed him.

Impulsively she moved toward him. A spare two steps were all it took to cover the distance between them. She touched his cheek with her fingertips, leaned up and kissed him. A brush of fairy wings, no more. Softness badly seemed to be missing from Max's life.

She sensed why he was so troubled. A man didn't work himself into a temper over clean socks unless there was a reason. An innocent smooch was still on his mind. An innocent smooch that had darn near turned into a conflagration under his yard light several nights ago. She'd tried denying those powerful feelings existed. Max hadn't. He knew what had happened and he wanted it buried. Six feet deep and the coffin closed.

Kitt knew herself to be vulnerable. She'd never understood that a man could be even more so. Max had simply been hurt too much, and she swore, silently, mentally and from her heart, that she wouldn't hurt him.

"We won't be in your way," she said softly, fiercely. "You'll never even know we're here."

She'd tricked him. Max didn't know how she'd done it, but she had.

Irritably he flipped the barn switch that started up the packing line. Immediately peaches gently rolled onto the sorting belt. The ones with blemishes were culled, and the best continued down the belt to be packed by size. At least that's what happened in an ideal world. "Moshe, see if she's still catching," Max yelled out.

"Got it, boss."

Max strode toward the main room in the barn, where workers were positioned around the revolving tables, waiting for the flow of peaches. With only one arm free, Max could do just so much with a wrench, and his mind was still on Kitt. It was those soft, blueberry-blue eyes that had tricked him. He'd started worrying about her leaving the baby, jumping into a new career too fast because she was desperate for money. If she stuck around, he could keep an eye on her.

Only, dammit, there was no way he needed an extra body to look after. Not in the summer. Not a woman. And never a lady who probably color coordinated her sneakers and didn't own a pair of jeans. He didn't want Kitt cooking for him, and he sure as hell didn't want her near his rancid socks.

From the end of the packing line, he had a window view of the office. Her head was bent over the payroll. Sunlight curled on the slender nape of her neck. The woman should have the sense to grow some hair so that too-naked, too-soft, too-vulnerable slope of neck wouldn't be exposed . . . and he hadn't liked that kiss. A hint of scent, a tease of taste, a softness, and his heart was still thudding, his veins still pumping adrenaline.

At least he assumed his veins were pumping adrenaline, because "danger" should be stamped in clear letters on Kitt's forehead. He would rather handle radioactive uranium. Kitt was far more trouble than that. She didn't seem aware of how strongly and disturbingly he was attracted to her, but he was. He also knew enough to avoid the kind of city woman whose values were totally alien to his.

The kind of woman Kitt was.

"I need a hand," Juan shouted.

"I'm there." Max swung around the corner and hunkered under the revolving table. Juan pointed to the moving gears. He started to explain what was wrong in the unique blend of Spanish and English they'd both mastered, then abruptly stopped talking. He just looked at Max and then the bundle Max was hauling around on his left shoulder.

Max didn't specifically remember taking the baby out of Kitt's arms, but Spike had been crying when he'd been trying to explain about the payroll. The payroll *had* to be done. There was never a spare moment for book work until after midnight, and in that sense—and only that sense—Kitt was an answer to a prayer.

Sort of.

An itsy-bitsy hand grabbed his earlobe. He winced. The tyke had nails like talons.

He'd spent months establishing authority and respect among his motley work crew. None of them were looking at him now, but he knew they were grinning at the Crest-Haven peaches rolling on the packing tables. Moshe passed by him to duck under the table and fix the sticking gear. He clapped a hand on Max's shoulder as if to comfort the demented.

A red pickup barreled in the yard to add to the confusion. Max's big hand tightened on the little one's fat behind as he strode outside. Clear as day, Kitt had promised that neither one of them would get in his way.

The spray consultant blinked at the sight of the baby. "Yours?" Harvey asked him disbelievingly.

There was no way, Max thought, absolutely none, that this could work out.

Kitt finished the payroll at five. Three times she'd left the desk to fetch Jennifer Lise, but Max—and her daughter—were still nowhere in sight. Moshe said something about a spray consultant coming in and Max needing a look at the Lorings.

"You mean he took the baby on a tractor?" Kitt couldn't believe it.

"I don't rightly know, ma'am, but my guess is that they took a truck."

"Without a car seat?"

"It's just a few hundred yards down the farm road, ma'am, and most of the time they'll just be walking around."

Kitt shook her head. "That's not the point. If Max had something—anything—he needed to do, he could have brought me the baby at any time. I've been right here!"

"Could be he didn't mind the baby with him, ma'am—although I ain't speaking for the boss."

Kitt directed a cool gray stare at the black-bearded bear standing next to her. "Moshe, if you 'ma'am' me one more time, you and I are going to come to blows. The name is Kitt. Got it?"

She caught the slow twist of a grin deep within the forest of black curling beard. Moshe's smile showed off his tobacco-stained teeth. He wore his belt just under the wad of stomach that rivaled her profile when she was seven months pregnant, and the sweat stains under his arms were big as moons.

He seemed an unlikely friend, and evidently he felt the same way about her, because he nervously shifted on his feet whenever she was around and had to clear his throat before he volunteered any conversation. "Were you going up to the house to make him some dinner, ma—Kitt?"

"I was thinking about it."

Moshe nodded. "He needs..." He hesitated. "Food. Regular food. I been working for him six years now. He took me in off the street, so I don't have much toleration for anybody criticizing him." He cleared his throat. "It's my considered opinion, though, that he'd be a lot less ornery if he had an occasional steak instead of an all-peanut-butter diet."

She had to fight a chuckle. "I'll keep that advice in mind, Moshe, but the man just stole my daughter. I'm really in no mood to spoil him."

"Steak," Moshe repeated blandly.

"Red meat is terrible for you."

"Steak," Moshe repeated one more time.

She didn't turn the T-bone under the broiler until she saw Max's pickup. The truck hurled and braked in the driveway with the speed of an emergency ambulance. The windows were open. Even if they'd been closed and storm shuttered, Kitt would have heard Lise's wail of hunger.

She hadn't started worrying until ten minutes before. As Kitt knew well, her daughter had an inner time clock where her bottle was concerned. A minute off the mark and pandemonium broke lose.

Max bolted through the back door with a panicked stride. "I know she *sounds* like I beat her and dragged her through the mud, but I swear she was fine until a few minutes ago—we were having a great time—"

"It's all right, Max, she's just hungry." Kitt already had a warmed bottle in her hand. She scooped the baby out of his arms and delivered the nipple.

When Lise immediately stopped crying, Max let out a gusty sigh of relief. He didn't look at her, though. Kitt understood. He may have uneasily agreed to her being around, but he wasn't going to risk her misunderstanding the ground rules. Max wasn't forming any attachments to any female older than two months.

"I finished the payroll," she said calmly. "I brought the checks in here for you to sign, and dinner's all ready."

"I'll pay you in cash right now..." Still standing in the back hall—lightning would probably strike if he came close to her—he delved into his back jeans pocket for his wallet. "But about dinner—I don't have time. Truck's due in. Have to call my broker before that, and there's a cultivator has to be fixed before tomorrow morning."

"I understand," she agreed. "There's no problem. I'll just throw the steak in the trash."

"Pardon?"

"Steak. It's rare now. It'll be medium in another few minutes. Much longer than that and it won't be fit for more than the trash. Still, if you don't have time, you don't have time. The sourdough rolls will probably keep; it's just that they get hard so quick, and baked potatoes are so rotten eaten cold...."

He stomped up the steps looking mad. And hungry. "I don't have time," he repeated gruffly.

"So you said. Heavens, who's arguing with you?" She added firmly, "I'll leave just as soon as Lise finishes her bottle. In fact, if we're in your way now, I could take her in the other room—"

"Just sit down. Right here." Where he could see her, he thought irritably. He could already see all the trouble she'd gone to. The table had a red-and-white checked tablecloth. He didn't own one. The silverware was all just so, and a delicate ceramic vase—heaven knew where she'd found that—was loaded with a mass of wildflowers. They'd die within hours. Kitt was such a city slicker she wouldn't know that you couldn't pick wildflowers. Kitt didn't sit down. Balancing the baby and bottle, she kept setting things in front of him. A baked potato, wallowing in sour cream and melted cheese. A fresh ear of corn, dripping butter. A broiled steak, huge, slathered with fresh mushrooms. Rolls, still steaming.

"Kitt, you just can't do this," he said uncomfortably.

"I like to cook, always have. I also like to play house, although I've never had much time to do it. Not full-time. I never wanted to wash windows full-time, but this has honestly been a treat for me."

He was not diverted. "These groceries weren't in the house yesterday."

Lise squirmed, letting Kitt know she had a burp. She shifted the baby to her shoulder and starting patting. "We made a run this morning."

"And how much did that little 'run' set you back?"

"One hundred and twelve dollars and forty-five cents."

He blinked.

"Your freezer was completely empty, and you obviously have no time to shop. It just made sense to stock up. But if you haven't got the cash, we'll call it a loan."

"Over my dead body we'll call it a loan." Between shoveled-in forkfuls, he pointed a finger at her. "You're not going anywhere until I've written you a check. And why aren't you eating?"

"I can eat at home."

"You should know there's enough here for ten people."

"Lise hasn't finished with her bottle."

"Then when she's finished. And I don't *believe* you didn't ask me for that money the minute you saw me this afternoon."

He was obviously still worried about the state of her bank account. If he'd known her better, Kitt knew he wouldn't be. Certainly she was unemployed and hadn't financially planned on keeping the baby, but she had caches and stashes of savings that had been ruthlessly hoarded for years. She was far too scared to ever be broke.

Money had always meant security to Kitt. Lately, though, the money that was supposed to make her feel safe simply wasn't doing its job. Maybe she had a screw loose. Anyone with a new baby should be more worried about money, not less.

Only the kind of security she wanted for Jennifer Lise couldn't be bought with money. And Kitt was increasingly afraid that she had badly, stupidly, blindly spent her adult lifetime pursuing nothing that mattered to her at all.

A white-sided semi rolled into the yard. Max stood up with a fork in one hand and a napkin in the other. "I have to go, but it'll only take me about fifteen minutes to load the truck. I'll write your check right after that. You don't have to leave any faster than that, do you?"

She shook her head.

He was out the door in a flash and halfway through the yard when he turned around. He stomped back to the open window and crossed his arms on the outside sill. "Ms. Sanders?"

His face was blurred by the screen. All she could see was his unruly shock of dark hair and the rare twist of a lazy grin.

"I just wanted you to know—that's the best meal I've ever had."

A ten-year-old could put together steak and a baked potato, but Kitt wasn't going to turn down the compliment. "Thank you, Mr. Carlson."

He rapped his knuckles on the sill. "Don't let Spike give you hell while I'm gone. And I expect to see you with your feet up when I get back in."

She didn't put her feet up. She perched on a corner of the table, holding Jennifer Lise, and watched Max greet the semi driver and then leap onto a forklift.

He was so gruff, so rough...so kind. Kitt tried to remember when she'd met a more compassionate man, and couldn't. Max leaped into everything he did with the same determination, the same vital energy, the same all-or-nothing commitment. He knew what he wanted. He knew what mattered to him. And he could match the toughness in the corporate moguls she'd once known, but Max was different. He had a heart as big as the sky.

Kitt set the baby carrier on the table so she could snatch a bite to eat while she handled the dishes. Guilt nagged her conscience. Conning the man into eating a decent dinner didn't bother her, but she'd allowed him to believe she was broke by being less than honest, and she'd played on his compassion to allow her to stick around and help him.

Trickery and dishonesty in women were the precise reasons Max was suspicious of the whole female species. All Kitt wanted was to be honest with him, yet he was the one who made that hard.

A woman who cared about Max, she considered thoughtfully, was always going to have to lead him a real slow dance.

It would take time for a woman to make Max believe he could count on her. Time to prove she wasn't using him. Time to make him believe that she had what it took to stand by him. And unless a woman did something to buy herself that kind of time, Max simply wouldn't give her a chance.

"Of course we're talking theoretically, Lise," she firmly told her daughter. "I've never chased a man in my life, and I'm hardly going to start now. All you and I are going to do is lend him a hand and stay completely—*completely*—out of his way. He needs a little lesson in trust, love, and you and I are in an ideal position to give it to him. He'll see. He's about to find out that there's at least one woman who would never cause him trouble."

Six

Kitt circled the riding lawn mower with the same wariness she would approach a prehistoric beast.

She'd been staring at Max's front-yard jungle for a week. The baby was napping in the house, which meant she needed to stay close but she had the time to mow his grass, assuming she could work up the courage.

Bending over the mower, she gingerly peered at the buttons and levers. There were the obvious whatcha-majiggies for the gas and gears and a lever to lower the blades. Nothing too alien there. She glanced at the motor. It looked like any other motor, a lot of ugly grease and coiled metal. She flipped the fuel cap and noted the tank was near empty, then narrowed her eyes at the fuel pumps at the far edge of the yard. If she drove it that far, she'd at least know if she could run the thing.

The sun baked her bare legs as she climbed on. Her white shorts and loose yellow pullover clung to her skin. It wasn't just hot; it was going-naked weather—not that she'd consider that option. Max was in the office, Moshe in the shop, and the whole yard was abuzz with people in motion.

She checked, but no one paid attention to the start of another motor over all the other noise. Carefully she slid the thing into gear and let out the clutch. It bucked like a burro—mastering the beast could conceivably take a little practice—but the mower obediently steered toward the fuel pumps.

She stopped and flipped the key, so smug-proud of herself that she couldn't stand it. Mastering a lawn-mowing tractor didn't necessarily rate pomp and parade, but all week she'd felt like a bumbling rookie. Laughing at herself had been easy—how could she possibly know anything about a farm?—but she couldn't help Max if she had to bother him every two seconds for advice.

She'd been doing her absolute best not to bother Max about anything.

Humming softly, she slipped off the seat and reached for the green-handled fuel nozzle. Someone shouted, but she didn't look up. Someone was always shouting around the barns, and she was busy unscrewing the gas cap. Both the cap and the nozzle smelled. She was trying to keep the fuel off her hands when she heard another voice yell out.

She glanced up and blinked. Max was racing toward her from the office, his forehead breaking out in sweat. Moshe was hurtling toward her from the shop, his big belly jiggling and his legs pumping hard. Three of Max's crew were barreling toward her in a straight line from the barn.

She was surrounded by a posse in a matter of seconds. All five men were panting and heaving and breathless. No one was looking her in the eye. Especially not Max.

Her heart sank clear to her toes. "Oh, Lord. What did I do?"

"Nothing, Kitt. Everything's fine," Max said calmly. He exchanged glances with Moshe, who carefully removed the fuel nozzle from her grasp. Then promptly took his three hundred pounds out of sight. Likewise, the three men from Max's crew turned on their heels and made fast tracks for the barn.

She was left alone with Max. The new Max. He looked exactly the same—dusty coal-black hair falling over his brow, a male voltage machine of energy, dark eyes out of a woman's fantasy, jeans that belonged in a ragbag. He was a good clone, but he wasn't her Max.

No matter how hard Kitt had tried not to bother him over the past week, they'd naturally crossed paths a hundred times—often enough over Jennifer Lise. Max had developed the habit of sneaking off with her daughter for an hour every day. With Lise, he came alive with emotion and laughter.

With Kitt, he'd become Mr. Sweet. Suddenly he'd forgotten all his cuss words. He never scowled, never snapped. She'd made enough city-rookie mistakes to make the average farmer roll with laughter, but not him. She could do no wrong. Everything she did was wonderful and appreciated. She could probably drop a rock on his head and he'd sweetly thank her.

Obviously, this was different—whatever she'd done had aroused half the farmyard—and although she had a sinking feeling in the pit of her stomach, she also felt a curious sensation of...relief. Proof Max was infinitely more natural than the cipher he'd turned into. She took another look at his fast-retreating staff.

"Why do I have the feeling they're trying to get out of earshot as quickly as possible?" she asked humorously.

"They're expecting me to raise hell with you," he admitted.

His tone was dry, but contrary to what she'd half hoped, there wasn't an ounce of hell in it. Kitt felt the brief, unconscionable urge to kick him in the keester—anything to get herself knocked off the idiotic pedestal he'd put her on—but one problem at a time. At the moment, her problem was complete confusion.

"I don't understand. They think you're going to be mad at me because I put gas in a lawn mower?" She shook her head disbelievingly. "Your workers have gone out of their way to be nice to me, Max, but this is ridiculous. I've used self-service pumps a zillion times for my car—"

"For gas," Max said patiently.

"Of course for gas."

"And the lawn mower uses gas." He motioned to the green-handled nozzle. "But that's diesel, sweetheart. And if you'd put that in the gas tank, I'd have been shopping for a new lawn mower tomorrow."

The color drained from her face. She wanted to protest that the pump didn't say diesel, but abruptly she saw that the huge green tank near the pump had the words printed in large block letters. And at a distance there was a red pump with a distinctly red-handled nozzle—obviously the one for gas. The difference was clear...to anyone familiar with fuel pumps.

She swallowed, hard. "I'm sorry, Max," she said lowly. "Go ahead and raise hell. I certainly would in your shoes."

"Don't sweat it. You've never been around a farm-yard before. How could you know?"

"I could have asked. I should have asked." Visions of his mountainous bills floated in her head. She'd nearly added the cost of a new lawn tractor to them. "How about if you boil me in oil and we call it square?"

She felt honestly terrible, until he smiled at her. It was one of those calm, considerate, caring smiles Max had been practicing on her all week. He started to say something, then checked himself—as if he had to control the impulse not to thank her for nearly destroying his tractor—and all she could think of was that this had gone far enough.

"There was no harm done," he said soothingly.

"But there could have been. Because of me. I know it's no excuse, but I was only trying to help."

"I know you were. And you've been a tremendous help, Kitt. Irreplaceable. So no more worrying about it, okay?"

* * *

Max stalked into the shop a few minutes later and snapped at Moshe, "Don't you say one word."

"Me? What makes you think I was going to say anything?" Moshe gave his full attention to a punctured tractor tire for at least two minutes. That was as long as he could conceivably keep quiet. "I sure thought I was going to see fireworks," he murmured amiably. "Not that you have a short fuse near anyone careless with machinery, but—"

"She wasn't being careless; she doesn't know anything about machinery. That makes it different. Subject closed."

"Hmm." But two minutes later, "She sure is a worker, that one."

"Shut up, Moshe."

"She pitches in headfirst, energy to burn, would probably give you the shirt off her back if it would help a body." He added genially, "She's gonna kill herself on that mower."

"Fine. *You* hog-tie her. There's no one who can talk that woman out of doing anything she wants to do." Max still had work waiting for him in the office, but finding himself diverted toward the shop was no surprise. He needed something physical to do. Like handling a hundred-pound tire. Or strangling a woman.

Hefting a crowbar in his hand, he backed up to where he could look through the doorway. He'd fueled the mower and showed Kitt how to use it, not because he wanted her to mow his lawn but because she was determined. Max had as much control over hail as he had over that woman when she had her mind set.

She was bucking around the yard at a pretty good clip. He'd instructed her to keep it in first gear. She was running it in third. Her hair was catching sunbeams, her skin glowing in the heat, her fanny bouncing on the seat. Something glistened in her ears, and if he weren't feeling so...agitated...he might have chuckled. Only Kitt would wear earrings to mow the lawn.

"She works pretty hard," Moshe observed again.

"She works like a dog," Max corrected him irritably. He thwacked the crowbar in his palm until Moshe removed it and applied it to the tractor tire.

"No reason for you to complain," Moshe said reasonably. "You're the only farmer in the county running around in starched white shirts...."

Max threw him a speaking glance.

"And as far as I know, you're also the only farmer with a newly waxed pickup...."

Max threw him another warning look. Kitt—out of the goodness of her heart—had decided to surprise him by cleaning his truck the other morning. She'd soaped, rinsed, resoaped, rerinsed, waxed, polished and then vacuumed the interior. And she'd been so happy with herself that there was nothing he could say. It had never occurred to her that he'd been stranded without his pickup for three hours that morning—or that a single ride down a farm road would make the truck look like a dustbin all over again.

"And I heard the boys say she put up some peaches for you yesterday...."

"Lay *off*, Moshe."

"I heard she picked some nice pretty Red Skins. Of course, I coulda sworn that variety wasn't gonna be ready to pick until next week...."

Max closed his eyes. Kitt had found about a hundred old canning jars in the basement, gotten so excited she couldn't stand it, took the baby out to the orchard and packed her car trunk full of peaches that were hard as rocks. To her, they looked just like the hard-as-rock peaches you bought in an urban grocery store. And she hadn't mentioned the fiasco to him until he had some thirty-six canned quarts of the greenest peaches he'd ever seen sitting on his counter when he'd come into dinner. God, she'd been happy, and prouder of herself than a Nobel prize winner.

"And it's not like she ain't got guts. Why, she took on Litowski like a hognose snake would take on a varmint...."

Again, Max winced. His buyer had driven in three afternoons ago. No one had been around but Kitt, who'd taken it in her sweet head to tell Sam Litowski that he should schedule his semis to pick up produce *before* the dinner hour. Kitt had the idiotic idea that farmers had to eat. And sleep.

Moshe had his hands full with the unwieldy tire. Max crouched next to him with a wrench, started to turn the lug nuts and then forgot them. Frowning, he backed up to check on her again. By some miracle she hadn't run into anything yet, hadn't killed herself, hadn't taken out any trees or bushes. When she went home—if she *ever* went home—he had to remember to get on the mower and pick up the wide swaths of grass she was missing.

He dragged a hand through his hair, watching her. Near anything she was familiar with, Kitt was a competent, take-charge wonder. She'd reorganized his record keeping in a matter of days, set up files that made sense, initiated a check-and-balance system so he had better day-by-day financial controls. He couldn't walk in the house when there wasn't a meal waiting for him, and the whole place was starting to shine. She did all that and took loving care of the baby without even breathing hard.

But that wasn't the stuff she *liked* to do.

She liked the farm. Poking around the tractors, the shop, the trucks, the orchards. Every time she poked she found some new way to "help him." Every time she found some new way to "help him," he found himself reaching for an antacid.

"Any day now, she'll get tired of it," Max murmured.

"Beg your pardon, boss?"

"It's only been two weeks. It just *seems* like three years. I keep telling her she doesn't owe me anything, but she won't listen, so why should I feel guilty? In fact, I've decided the kindest thing I can do is just let her run until she gets sick of it all on her own."

"I still ain't following. What's she supposed to get sick of?"

"The farm. It's the newness, you understand. Never met a city woman who didn't fall in love with the *idea* of country. You know—fresh air, trees, land... especially land. They *all* get that Scarlett O'Hara thing about land."

"Scarlett O'Hara?" Moshe squinted at him blankly.

"They *think* the land's romantic...until they get the first squish of real mud between their toes. Kitt will come around. A few more bug bites, a few more blisters, daily exposure to the bills it takes to run this place—I'm not going to push her. I won't have to. The farm season'll be over in a few more weeks. It shouldn't take her that long to figure out she'd rather be on the leather upholstery of a BMW than a tractor seat." He heard the distant grating of a gear being stripped and patted his shirt pocket. There was one antacid left. He'd started the morning with a full roll.

Moshe took the wrench out of Max's hand since he wasn't using it. "Somehow I had the idea that you were hoping she and the tyke might stick around."

"There was never any chance of that," Max said flatly.

"Seems like there's more baby gear around your place than furniture."

"I borrowed things from my sisters. If she's determined to spend so much time here, I had to do something. She was hauling a truckload of strollers and playpens and whatall from her cottage every morning." He added, "It'll all go back when she's out of here."

"I coulda sworn you were a mite attached to the little one."

"The howling coyote?" Max scoffed, and then sighed. "Yeah, I am."

"I coulda also sworn—" Moshe straightened "—that you were just a mite attached to her mother."

Max's head snapped around. "Good God, no. It's nothing like that."

"No?"

"Of course not. It's just that she and the baby don't have anyone else right now. Hell, she just had her life turned upside down. It's no surprise that she needs a little space and time to get on her feet again. I think of her..." Max probed his mind for the appropriate word. "I think of her like a sister."

"A sister," Moshe echoed.

"A sister," Max repeated.

The rumble started in Moshe's belly, rollicked through his diaphragm and erupted through his throat in the form of a guffaw. This from the man Max had taken off the street six years before, dried out, fed, cleaned up and given a job. There was loyalty for you. Moshe was laughing so hard he needed both beefy palms to wipe the tears spattering from his eyes.

Thoroughly disgusted, Max stomped out of the shop.

For two cents, he'd fire Moshe. Following that line of reasoning, unfortunately, he'd have to fire the entire crew.

No one said anything, but there wasn't a man on the farm who didn't look after her when Max was tied up. They all knew he was nuts about her. Even *he* knew he was nuts about her, but the metaphorical reference to lunacy was certainly relevant.

He hadn't sworn off women out of bitterness but because he had an undeniably bad history of being attracted to women with no staying power. Kitt was not of his world, not of his values. Her attraction to the farm was temporary. She was as vulnerable as crystal right now, alone, groping for a peaceful space of time in a life that had shifted priorities on her. In

Max's view, a man who'd take advantage of a vulnerable woman was scum. No exceptions. No excuses.

But when they were close she stirred him up like a witch's pot of magic. She made him laugh. She made him think, and there was no question she made him feel. He couldn't sleep for thinking about her skin, the tilt of her lips when she smiled, the husky murmur of her voice. Her small, elegant fanny. Her long, long legs....

Kitt had to get sick of helping him soon.

She just had to.

When he drove into the yard that evening it was past seven, and he was relieved to find her car gone. There were no semis due tonight, nothing pressing that he had to handle beyond an imminent case of starvation. He strode through the back door, feeling guilty that he hoped she'd left him something on the stove.

He looked up, but there was nothing. No simmering pot, no savory smells, no prissily set table with a napkin lined just so... no sassy blonde with her chin in the air, determined to con him into eating when he made token protests about not having time.

He washed his hands in the back bathroom, meeting his eyes in the mirror's reflection. *She was spoiling you silly, Carlson. And you have no business feeling disappointed.*

He told himself he didn't feel disappointed, but when he shut off the water taps, the whole house rang with silence. No baby's wail, no woman's voice, just that silence, as thick as lead and as loud as loneliness.

He didn't notice the note until he climbed the three steps to the kitchen. Her scrawl was just like Kitt—

hard to read and distinctly, dangerously feminine: "Dinner's ready at the pond."

That quickly, his pulse picked up the nag of anticipation. That quickly, he started worrying what she was going to put him through this time that would tear him inside out.

Kitt stood up, holding Lise, when she saw Max's pickup round the corner of the orchard. Her skin was flushed, her heart beating with nervousness.

She'd decided after the diesel/gas episode that enough was enough. It was one thing for Max to be understanding of a mistake and another for him to tiptoe around her as though she would break from a cross word. If having her around upset him too badly, she had to either leave—and quickly—or do something to reduce the tension between them.

The dinner had taken some thought, but the setting had been easy to choose. She'd discovered the pond on the day she picked peaches with the baby. She'd stepped away from the last tree in the row and there it was ... a huge stand of virgin woods, green and shadowy and cool, leading down to a diamond-shaped pond bordered with water lilies.

It was a place of magic, even for a woman who could have sworn she no longer believed in it. Sun danced off the water with the sheen of opals, and the pond was set in a low vale, where the scent of peaches had settled like a heady perfume. The grassy bank was shaded by an old silver maple, its leaves glinting like sterling with the least breath of breeze.

For years Kitt had had an original oil painting over her desk, a landscape of a lake. She adored the painting, had carted it with her from office to office. The first moment she saw Max's pond, she knew the painting for the sham it was. One was fake, the other real. Disturbingly, it struck Kitt that she'd settled for the fake for too long.

Max hadn't. For Max, it was the real thing or nothing. The pond was cached in the middle of his farm like a secret—his secret. He could have felled the woods and made the land arable. He hadn't. He used the pond water for irrigation, but he'd left the grassy banks and woods alone. A practical man with a knowledge of his debt load would have made other choices. Max was a practical man. He knew damn well what he owed the bank.

So he obviously loved this spot. Unbearably.

Or so she was counting on.

Max never drove slower than a bat out of hell, and tonight was no exception. He braked, bolted from the truck and strode toward her with an electric energy that defied the weather—the night was hotter than a firecracker—and Kitt's hold tightened on the baby as his gaze swept the makings of her picnic.

Either he'd react as she hoped, or her whole dinner was going to flop like limp spaghetti.

A plain old blanket had been laid on the grassy bank, but over that was a French linen tablecloth—white, to match the china. Champagne cooled in a sterling silver ice bucket. The label was Moët, and mounds of Russian roe on crackers were the hors d'oeuvre—neither item easy to find in a farmer's town.

Max was squinting too hard for her to read his expression—the evening sun hit him smack in the eyes—but she was almost sure she saw his mouth twitch. Encouraged, she crouched down and lifted the lids off hot plates so he could see the rest. Wild rice and smoked ham with cashews was the main course; pairs of asparagus tips had been elegantly wrapped in orange slices; the sorbet had been difficult to cool, and peach melba was the dessert. Jennifer Lise was only wearing a diaper, in deference to the heat, but her single tuft of hair was pinned with a white satin bow.

Max shook his head, traced the baby's satin bow with his finger and met her eyes in a dance of fire and flint. "You're nuts, woman."

Kitt's lungs abruptly released a pent-up sigh. She could see Max was cautious—plenty cautious—but his eyes were crinkled in dry humor and his roguish mouth was crooked in a grin. "I owed you for nearly wrecking your tractor this afternoon."

"You never owed me anything. How many times do I have to tell you?" He waggled his fingers—a familiar signal—and she turned the baby over to him.

Sometime she was going to have to tell him that the average man who worked a killingly physical day had no interest or energy for babies. Not now. Her daughter settled upside down on his forearm like a happy football, and Kitt needed both her hands free to handle the champagne. "We won't call this dinner 'owing' then," Kitt agreed. "We'll just call it necessary."

"Necessary?" His gaze again whisked over the French linen and caviar.

"Now don't get scared off just because it isn't pot roast. I may not know diesel from gas, but a formal touch at dinner is a yuppie's area of expertise. And after watching me bumble around your farm all week—"

"Hey, you've been doing okay," he immediately defended her.

Actually she thought she was doing okay, too, for an Eskimo suddenly dropped in the desert. Max was the one who'd lost his sense of laughter, which had led her to questioning why, and her crazy picnic had seemed an answer of a kind. He was never nervous when she acted like a city woman. His defenses only went on red alert when she was trying to fit in—to his life, to him. Heaven forbid she should try to get close.

Tonight, Kitt had every intention of getting close to Max—as a friend. Her hormones had been banished to the attic, her physical awareness of him packed away, her pulse programmed to stay on neutral. If she cared much more for Max than as a friend, that was her problem. It was never supposed to be his. "I've been worried about you," she told him frankly.

"Worried? Why?"

She backed a safe distance away as she started to twist the cork on the champagne. "You work hard—terribly hard—for this land, Max, and I'll bet you fly by this pond a dozen times on a summer day. It's your irrigation source, right? And maybe you have to get practical about it, but it occurred to me that it might have been a while since you took an hour off to smell the roses. In case you haven't had the time to notice, this is an idyllic hideaway."

"Kitt?"

"Hmm?" The cork popped and foam bubbled out all over her fingers. She licked it off before ducking under the maple's branches for her picnic basket. Somewhere she'd packed two fluted crystal glasses.

"I'm not a romantic man. Words like *idyllic* and *hideaway* aren't even in my vocabulary." He watched her tongue lap the edge of her finger and felt every muscle tighten. He just felt safer warning her against certain kinds of expectations.

"Carlson?"

"Hmm?"

"This isn't a tête-à-tête. It's a cultural exchange. I get to enjoy champagne in bare feet. You get to taste caviar in jeans. But that's all. Words like *seduction* and *moonlight* were wiped out of my vocabulary a long time before I met you...if by any chance you were worried this was a setup."

"That never crossed my mind."

"And horses fly." Kitt handed him a glass brimming with champagne, cheerfully bussed him on the forehead and pointed to his feet like a schoolmarm. "Now that we have that settled—off with the boots. Mother Sanders is about to give you a fast lesson in the art of relaxing, starting with sipping the champagne with our feet in the water."

"Relaxing?"

"Poor baby, didn't you recognize the word? I can tell we're going to have to start your education from scratch. You probably can't even spell the word *lazy*— and why are those boots still on?"

Max chuckled. Maybe it was the cheeky way she'd pecked his forehead; maybe it was her sassy way of calling a spade a spade as far as her intentions for this dinner were concerned, but he relaxed. Only Kitt didn't. Over the next hour, he watched her ardent promises of a lazy dinner go up in smoke. It didn't bother him, but it obviously bothered Kitt.

She was giving him a lesson in caviar and wooden spoons when their peace disappeared. Lise always knew when Kitt picked up an eating utensil, any eating utensil. The little tyke didn't like her mother to eat and couldn't stand a quiet dinner.

Within an hour, the huge red sun had dropped into the pond, turning the sky into jeweled colors and the water into a mirror. The sunset was the stuff of romance. Kitt never saw it. She was too busy pacing, balancing urchin and plate.

Max shoveled down dinner so he could relieve her. The screamer quieted down when he fed her a bottle, but the wails started up again when Kitt tried to diaper her. Eventually the dishes were stashed in the back of his truck, and after that they both took turns walking the little insomniac.

None of it bothered Max, but he could hardly tell Kitt he was having a wonderful time. He could see the distress and anxiety on her face. Her dinner had gone down the tubes—it was for his sake that that mattered to her—and he was moved, more than he wanted to admit, by seeing her in the role of mother. She was wonderful with Lise—endlessly patient, soothing, nurturing, loving.

But the little brat very honestly did better thrown over a male shoulder. Kitt had burped the darling with gentle little pats. Max smacked the gas bubbles out of her and that was that.

Kitt assumed she'd done something wrong because the baby was fretful. That was horseradish, but there was no way he could explain how he knew that. A

grown man could hardly talk about something as
vague as a psychic bond—but it was there. Lise hated
to sleep. So did he. She was a stubborn, snub-nosed
squaller who screamed for absolute hell when a breath
of wind rubbed her the wrong way. Max knew damn
well they didn't have the same genes, but he had the
same genetic flaw. And Lise was not averse to staging
a tantrum if it would successfully claim her mother's
complete attention.

Max wasn't into staging tantrums; he was into de-
nial, but if the cuff side of his heart was exposed . . .
he felt the same way about garnering her mother's attention.

Eventually the urchin had to give in. When her lids
drooped and she nestled into Kitt's chin, Kitt looked
up at him. "Is she gone?"

"Dead gone," he whispered.

"You're sure? I can't see her face."

"I'm sure."

"Max, be *sure*. Once she's out, she's down for the
count. But if I try to lay her down before she's sleeping, we could go through this all over again."

"Sweetheart, she's out like a power plant failure.
Trust me."

Kitt had already set up a playpen in the shade of an
old hickory. Slowly and carefully, she laid down the
baby and then covered the pen with mosquito net-
ting. By then the sky was jet black and studded with
stars. Max had folded up her French linen tablecloth
but left the blanket. It was a good thing, because she
came out of the shadows looking for a place to crash.
She sprawled next to him like such an exhausted zom-
bie that he had to smile.

"Tell me you don't go through that every night," he murmured.

"She's usually an angel—"

"I've heard that one before. You can only sell me wooden nickles once, honey."

Eyes closed, she backpedaled closer to the truth. "It's just occasionally at dinnertime."

"It'll pass. I've seen it with my sisters' kids. Another month and you won't even remember this."

"I want that in blood, Carlson. Furthermore, I'm dying of humiliation. We gulped down the caviar, shoveled in the sorbet; the ham was cold. You were supposed to relax. You work so hard, Max."

He felt something still inside of him. She cared about him. Really cared, dangerously cared. That was never supposed to happen, and he'd worked impossibly hard to keep his distance so it couldn't.

Somehow he'd let it all slip. His layers of caution weren't thick enough. Not tonight. He had a feeling of family with her that he'd never had. His bond with the urchin was part of that, but the dynamite level of trouble related to his feelings for Kitt alone. All evening he'd felt like her husband. Her mate.

And she'd been with him as if he were the one man in her life she trusted, shared with, knew she could count on. Max counted on no one. Not anymore. Luring him, shaking him, was the knowledge that Kitt didn't, either. Except with him.

He didn't know what to do about it . . . but he knew damn well that lying next to Kitt on a blanket in the dark was a temptation he was far too close to taking. "You hot?" he murmured.

"Pardon?"

"The baby's sound asleep. It has to be a hundred and ten. The pond is cold like you can't believe, but the water's clean and you can dive off the bank. It's only shallow near the lily pads; the rest is twenty feet deep."

"Pardon?" She'd turned her head but she still looked blank.

"Can't you swim?"

"Sure I can swim, but—" She snapped quick to her elbows when she saw him shucking off his shirt and reaching for the snap on his jeans.

"We tried relaxing city-slicker style, honey. It's about time we gave it a country go. Skinny-dipping is as much a time-honored custom in the country as caviar in the city."

"Max—"

"Strip. And if I were you I'd do it quick, because you're going to get wet at the count of twenty whether you have clothes on or not."

"Max—"

"One. Two. Three—"

Seven

It wasn't the swimming Kitt objected to. It was the
stripping.

"Six. Seven—"

She hadn't set up the dinner to...entice him. The
opposite was true. She owed Max and she'd found a
way to pay him back. If Max could be coaxed to believe that one woman wouldn't let him down, his
lonely house of suspicious cards might come tum-
bling down. She wanted nothing from him. Just the
chance to be that friend. Her motives were saint-pure,
completely altruistic and righteously honorable.

Mostly.

"Thirteen. Fourteen—"

He flashed past—no embarrassment whatsoever—
and she saw his muscled body spear in a dive. He surfaced with a sleek wet head and a grin full of mis-

chief, his naked shoulders glistening by starlight. So much for altruism and righteousness. The first glimpse of his bare tush made her heart beat like a lusty, pagan drum. A saint would be horrified at the carnal tingles chasing down her spine.

"Eighteen, Ms. Sanders. Come on, come on. I guarantee I'm not the only one getting wet here and if I have to come out there and get you—"

Well, damn him.

She peeled off her shorts and underpants at the same time. That should have been the hardest part, but pulling off her blouse was the hardest part. Her wonderfully loose yellow blouse hid a multitude of flaws. Courtesy of Lise, her stomach was still pudgy. Courtesy of age, her breasts had developed an unfortunate new relationship with gravity. It wouldn't have mattered if Max had been sweet and averted his eyes.

Max was a cad. He had his hands on his hips in the chest-deep water and was staring right at her.

"Nineteen—"

She never took off the bra. She told herself there wasn't time. Her bare feet skidded on the bank and then she dived, blindly, fast. The water was gasping cold, black as ink and wonderfully concealing.

Unfortunately, when she came to the surface she found herself attacked. Not by Max, by lily pads. The delicate flowers were white and fragrant, but beneath the water were millions of root tendrils that clung to her skin. In the next life, maybe she'd have the foresight to look before she dived.

Max saved her from the junglelike vines by catching her wrist and pulling her into deeper water. "You could have been hurt," he scolded. "The only place it's shallow in the whole pond is by the lilies." He plucked a last flat green leaf from her hair with a grin designed to ransom a woman's common sense. "And what's this?"

"What's what?" But she knew what. His forefinger had lifted the shoulder strap of her bra.

"You can skinny-dip in your underwear, but you'd get labeled a permanent woos. You don't want that."

She saw his eyes, black as the devil's, then felt his fingers tug at the hook in back. She ducked, but the lacy trace of white lingerie was already floating free.

"Better," Max said with satisfaction, and then looked at her. "Not better? Good grief, woman, you look like you just swallowed a lemon. Since when are you nervous around me?"

"I'm not nervous. I'm never nervous," she assured him, but Max wasn't listening to her. He slicked a hand through his wet hair and frowned.

"When's the last time you played?"

"Played?"

"You put that dinner together for me. That was a lot of work. You set *me* up to relax, but I've yet to see you sit still from the day I met you. When's the last time you played—really played? Horsed around, cut up, forgot your worries and just plain let down your hair?"

Kitt stared at him blankly. A glass of champagne. That's all he'd had. Hardly enough to explain his asking such silly questions. She was no child. He knew that. He also knew she was too old to "horse around," too mature to ever completely forget her responsibilities. Especially since the baby, she simply couldn't afford to be less than serious. Ever.

Max ducked under the water and nipped her thigh. Hard.

She yelped in shock and lost her footing. When she sliced to the surface again, she was in deep water and Max was dog-paddling next to her. His sudden disgracefully wicked grin was gone; he looked repentant. She thought he was going to apologize. Instead, she felt a palm cup her bare fanny and squeeze.

She shrieked, then scissor-kicked and sprang into a racing crawl. She covered the length of the pond before she was forced to raise her head gasping for air.

He was nowhere. The black night was silent, stars peppering the churned-up surface of the pond. She turned around, searching wildly—nothing. Her lungs heaved a sigh of relief, and then she felt the tweak of her nipple. A brazen tweak. A brazen, sexy, evocative, erotic tweak.

His head popped out of the water. He made the mistake of trying to draw in air through a mouthful of grin. There was no time to make a cautious, rational, careful decision, and she didn't. She surged out of the water and applied both hands ruthlessly to the top of his head. He went down—good and down—but she didn't waste any time taking off.

He caught her.

She let him.

And then she caught him, and he let that happen—it was a game. The kind of game teenagers play, only Kitt had never been a carefree teenager. She'd been too scared of being broke all her life to ever do anything so irresponsible as...flirt. Play. Tease.

Except with Max. The night was hot, and the pond nestled in the sable-dark woods. No one could hear their splashing antics; no one could hear their exhilarated laughter. Max added enough spice to make her feel good and wicked, but there was no harm. With him, there never had been. Only with him had Kitt ever felt the freedom to just be herself. Only with him had she ever felt . . . trust. The kind of real trust that a woman dreamed of finding with a man and never, ever, believed she would.

They finished a fast race the length of the pond that made her blood rush, her heart pound. She was just slicking back her dripping hair when Max surged up behind her.

"Hey. You're supposed to let the guy win. Didn't you learn anything in seventh grade?"

She chuckled. "Poor baby. It hurts to be shown up by a woman, doesn't it?"

"Darn tootin' it hurts—and you never learned to swim like that in any executive boardroom."

"Lunch hours at the Y. Swimming was always my stress release," she confessed, and suddenly caught her breath.

Max meant nothing by the game. She'd been sure. The night was unbearably warm and skinny-dipping nothing out of the ordinary for a farmer with a pond. Max was a physical man and they were, after all, adults. A little slap and tickle on a night as dark as pitch was hardly the same thing as intentional seduction. Max hadn't laid a hand on her in all this time. She was the one plagued with a mortifying one-sided physical awareness.

Or so she'd believed, until the throaty sound of his laughter faded. His eyes met hers, and she was suddenly aware that her breasts showed under a bare layer of water. He never looked below her neck, but for the briefest moment his gaze froze on hers. And on a calm, cloudless night there was suddenly lightning.

The moment was over faster than an eye blink...and so was their play. "Enough for me. Hell, you play rough, woman," he complained. "You wore me out."

"I wore *you* out?"

"Yeah, you. Just stay right there. It'll take me two shakes to pull on my jeans, and then I'll bring you the tablecloth for a towel."

She stayed, crouched in the shadows where the water lapped at her shoulders, watching Max heave up the bank and stomp over to his jeans. Water trickled down his skin, catching where his skin was teak dark above his waist and cream below it.

Even in a hurry—and Kitt could see that he was suddenly in a fast hurry to get clothes on—he showed no self-consciousness about his body. His legs were long cords of roped muscles, his shoulders and upper arms more of the same, and his face... When he turned toward her again, the expression on his face was as hard and unyielding as granite.

Granite with a smile. His jeans were zipped but not buttoned when he snatched up the white tablecloth and walked toward her with it spread out like a sheet. She saw the sheet but couldn't take her eyes off that so deliberate smile. "I can hear your teeth chattering from here. Come on." He held up the cloth so his face was blocked from the other side. "Nobody's peeking. Nothing to get nervous about. We're just going to get you warm and dry."

He'd done it before, she thought fleetingly. Gone out of his way to say something to make her feel safe and secure. But at the moment he was working at it too hard.

She shivered wildly when she stepped out of the water and felt that first contact of night air against her wet skin. Max immediately swaddled her in the bulky cloth. An edge fell off her shoulder. Instantly he jerked it back, covering her completely, and used another edge to dry her tousled wet hair. His touch was protective, brotherly.

And his teeth were clamped together as if he were fighting off a fever.

"Max," she murmured. He'd whipped around behind her. If he rubbed her shoulders any harder, he was going to tear off skin. She was slightly chilled but hardly suffering hypothermia, and it had never occurred to her that swimming together had been a test for Max. That touching her in any way was a test for Max. A test he was determined to pass or die trying.

"You look like a wet rat, but not to worry. I'll have you warm again in no time."

"Max."

"Next time you want to play, remind me to start a game that works on dry land. You should have warned me you swim like a porpoise."

"Max."

But he didn't look at her. Like a kid too scared to face the boogeyman in the closet, he shifted, while his gaze sought then landed on something safe. Jennifer Lise. Kitt already knew her daughter didn't need checking on, partly because she'd already checked on her a half dozen times and partly because Lise slept like a mummy once she was finally out. Max knew that, too, but he was determined to pursue the distraction. "She still wakes up for a last bottle, doesn't she? It's late. I'll bet she's going to wake up any minute."

Sometimes Lise woke for a last bottle, sometimes not. Either way, Kitt had no doubt about her daughter's ability to let the entire world know if she had even the smallest problem.

She wasn't worried about Lise. She was worried about Max. She freed her hand from the smothering tablecloth, lifted her palm and turned his whiskered cheek away from the view of the playpen and back to her.

He didn't look at her as if he saw a wet rat or a porpoise. He caught her palm sliding away from his cheek. Caught it and captured it, with his thumb on the pulse of her wrist, and he only said one word. "No."

For the briefest moment she studied the fire in his eyes, the compressed line of his lips, the yank of hair dripping on his forehead. She thought of all the times women had been accused of saying no when they really meant yes. She thought of all she had to lose— dignity and pride—and then she thought of what Max was afraid of losing. Dignity and pride. And she reached for him.

Her lips brushed his, wet and cool and slow. Real slow. Her tongue slid along his upper lip with infinite tenderness, then gave his lower lip the same attention. He tried to move...but he didn't try very hard. Her palms framing the sides of his face were enough to hold him still, and her thumb stroked, soothing the hot beating pulse in his throat. When he tried to say something she claimed another kiss, not with brazen assertiveness but with thorough, devastating care.

That was it. He murmured something low and gruff...he was probably telling her no again...but his body delivered a completely different message. His mouth claimed hers, not once, but over and again. He tasted clean and male and heady, and he kissed her until her lips ached, until every nerve ending had his name on it, until a sense of belonging—to him, with him—shimmered through her bloodstream.

And so did desire. When she wound her arms around his neck, the tablecloth slid and then caught somewhere around her waist. She didn't care. His eyes had the shine of ebony; his whole body was taut with need. She knew Max cared, but not this much, not this way.

His chest hair, rough and scratchy, rubbed against the soft skin of her breasts. The contrast electrified senses already humming with voltage. Feeling voltage around Max was familiar. Feeling loved wasn't. Feeling treasured and cherished, feeling an emotion so huge it filled up her throat...how many thousands of mistakes had she made in this lifetime?

Not this one.

If loving Max was a mistake, she'd throw in the towel. She wanted him, but the far more luring temptation was his need to be loved, wanted, needed. Max wasn't supposed to be human. Max wasn't supposed to need anyone. Max wasn't ever going to let himself be weak again,

Lava trapped under enough pressure always blew. She would have been scared if it had been any other man. He plucked the last of the tablecloth draping her thighs and hurled it, then leveled an openmouthed kiss on her and took her down . . . down where the grass made a ticklish bed and he could hold her. Length to length. Naked chest to naked chest.

She felt his fingers slide through her hair, deepening an embrace that was already out of control. A sound came out of her throat, forced from the rush of his hand down her spine, the depth of his tongue searching hers, the earthy feel of his arousal. It wasn't what she knew, this wild catapulting into sensation. She assumed Max wasn't aware of what he was doing to her, that he was simply caught up in emotions too long suppressed. She was wrong.

He slowed down, cruelly, deliberately. He lifted his head and leisurely studied her white breasts, so leisurely that she felt an anxious restlessness. She didn't want him to look.

And then he dipped his head and nuzzled her nipple. His lips closed on the dark tip, tasting with his tongue, then his teeth. His palm cupped and kneaded the surrounding swell of flesh as if he'd just discovered a treasure. When his hand slipped down to her abdomen and gave it the same reverent attention, she saw his eyes. He knew. He knew she felt vulnerable about her not-so-young body . . . and he used that knowledge, ruthlessly and with unbearable sensitivity, to make her burn.

A star fell on the western horizon. Neither noticed. In the woods, branches shaped like broccoli, gnarled and curved, silhouetted shadow on shadow. The pond stilled, reflecting a carpet of stars. And Kitt found the only man who had ever, could ever, strip away the civilized layers that had protected her for years.

She was a woman for him, incapable of being more, unwilling to be less. Desire clawed through her, making her breathless, making her ache. She'd been naked with a man before, but never like this. With her lips, her tongue, her body, her hands, she caressed him with the same wild ardor he showed her...only with Max, it felt natural. With Max, it felt right. If he made it impossible for her to hide anything from him, he was equally honest—and demanding—with her.

Max knew he was courting an edge. His sandpaper chin grazed her cheek and then he kissed her again. His tongue drove, seeking a mate and finding hers. She tasted as if she were made for him. The texture of her skin, her scent, her long legs rubbing against his— she felt as if she were part of him. Or could be.

His hand swept down to her breast. So foolish. She was so foolishly sensitive about her body, and realizing that was when he'd first lost his head. She was golden and precious and beautiful. Someone had to show her that. Someone also had to show her that a perfect body had nothing to do with passion. Passion was about emotion. When a woman burned for a man, yielded as if she was his whole world, responded as though she'd die if she couldn't touch him...that was what a man dreamed of.

Max had dreamed of it all his life. He'd never dreamed, never imagined, Kitt. Every muscle in his body was as coiled as a lariat. He wanted to take her. She wanted to be taken. Outside of two seconds he could be driving inside of her, her slim legs wound round him, her throat arched, both of them soaring toward satisfaction.... He was damn sure Kitt didn't know what good sex was. He would make it good for her.

Assuming he was bastard enough to do it.

Roughly, too roughly, he clutched her shoulders and broke off a kiss that had already tested the limits of his control. He rolled away, his lungs heaving in air louder than a freight train. His eyes tried to focus on the skyful of stars. Even when he closed his eyes he still saw those stars. And every stupid one of them had her name on it. God, how could he have let things go so far?

All week he'd watched her on the farm like a diamond in a tinsel factory. She didn't belong. Not here and not with him, and making love might appease a momentary need . . . but it would only create a greater one.

She was going to break his heart when she left. He already knew that. He also knew that she *was* going to leave him, and he'd be damned if he was going to face his shaving mirror every morning, knowing he'd taken advantage of a vulnerable woman.

"Max?"

He didn't respond, and for a moment Kitt couldn't seem to move. The last she remembered, they'd been close to Lise's playpen, his truck, her car and the last traces of a picnic in the shade of a maple tree. Now, all of those things were shadows in the distance.

Kitt wasn't in the habit of wantonly rolling in the grass, much less of losing all sense of time and place. Her mouth felt bruised and sensitive, and her whole body was still throbbing, tuned to Max, humming the love song Max had started.

She hadn't wanted to stop.

She still didn't.

Less than steadily she rose up on an elbow, automatically checked on her soundly sleeping daughter yards away... and then turned her complete attention to Max.

He was in trouble. So much trouble that her gaze softened and she buried her own feelings of need and frustration. He'd lurched to a sitting position and drawn up his knees. Unsatisfied desire might be responsible for his hard breathing, but it didn't begin to explain the taut anxiety in his expression. His profile was harsh and bleak, his spine more rigid than a ledge.

She said the only thing she could. "It's all right."

"The hell it is. You trusted me."

It seemed the oddest time to realize she was hopelessly in love with him. "I still do."

"I had no birth control protection."

"And that's why you stopped?"

"Hell, no." His head swiveled around, and she saw his eyes. "Neither of us are wet behind the ears. A man with any creativity at all can find a way to please a lady without putting her at risk." His bluntness was familiar, but the raw edge in his voice was not. "You told me about those skinny tubes, but the chance was still there. I'd never have put you at risk, Kitt. Not ever—without asking you."

"I don't doubt that," she said softly.

"Making love would have been a different kind of risk. I knew how you felt. I've guessed how you felt every time you looked at me. So it was up to me to make sure this didn't happen."

She thought that she'd hid her feelings for him brilliantly, but at the moment her pride seemed an expendable commodity. "It bothers you...that I care about you?"

She hadn't used a terrifying word like *love*, but even so, Max bolted to his feet. He tramped through the grass until he found the tablecloth, brought it back and gently draped it around her shoulders.

"You're not going to be a farmer's wife, Kitt," he said quietly. "I have nothing to give you. Not security, not stability—not any of the things you value. Not any of the things you need with the baby. When you're looking at things a little more clearly, you'll know it's true—I have nothing in hell you want."

He turned away again, moving from shadow to shadow until he retrieved his shirt and work boots. She should start finding her own clothes—it was late; she knew they were leaving—yet she couldn't seem to make herself move.

His "I have nothing you want" tore at her. He honestly seemed to believe it...that he had nothing to offer a woman, and least of all her. Max was completely wrong about what she valued, but until that moment she hadn't realized how deep his scars were.

Once before, he'd admitted to having needs and vulnerability. That was when his ex-wife had cut out, and Kitt mulled over how harshly he'd taken that lesson. In every encounter she and Max had ever had, he'd been protective and considerate of her feelings—never his own. His needs, his wants, his emotions were never mentioned. It was as if they didn't matter—not anymore—not to him.

"It's hard for you to believe I would want to stay," she murmured. "No woman's ever stayed for you, have they, Max? The easy times were no test, but when the going got a little rough, you never found anyone you could count on—''

"And neither have you." Still buttoning his shirt, he leaned over and pressed a kiss on her brow. A kiss of fierce, hard tenderness. "I'm not going to hurt you. I want you like hell. Now you know. But that doesn't mean that I would do anything, ever, to hurt you."

"What if I'm not asking for that kind of protection?"

"Then you should be."

It was touchy to argue with a man whose values about honor where women were concerned were relics from cavemen times. "Carlson, I'm thirty-nine years old," she said gently. "Don't you think it's conceivably possible that I can figure out all by myself what I want, what I feel, what I need?"

He didn't smile, although she meant the question to sound teasing. "You do that a lot—bring up your age—like you think it's living proof that you're a real experienced toughie. You keep forgetting that I was with you that night on the road. It never once occurred to you—never once—that anyone would stand by you. That says it all as far as your 'vast' experience. What the hell kind of men have you been involved with?"

She said softly, "Men who weren't you."

"That's sex talking," he said bluntly.

Color flooded her cheeks. Max couldn't see it in the darkness, but she guessed that was what he wanted. Not necessarily to make her blush, but to divert her from the dangerous track the conversation was taking. He definitely didn't want to hear that she loved him. What troubled her far more was that Max, very possibly, didn't believe anyone could love him.

"A woman couldn't just...want you...could she? Apart from sexual feelings. I mean you. The man. Who you are, what you are, what you value, all of it."

"Lift your arms." She had to drop the tablecloth to obey him. He threaded the neck of her yellow blouse over her head the way he would have dressed a child. Only he didn't look at her like she was a child. He looked at her as if she was as dangerous a temptation as Eve. "I've been around too many blocks to mistake emotions for what they're not. Sex is damned powerful. So is need, so is loneliness—and so is being scared."

She whispered, "You're right about that. There are a lot of things I'm afraid of."

"I know."

"I'm afraid most," she admitted, "of making any more mistakes. I can't lose anymore, Max. In fact, the only way I would take another emotional risk is if I were absolutely sure in my heart that it was right." She said it like a promise, but that wasn't the way he took it.

"Sweetheart, I *know*. I understand. I've been there." His eyes were a blaze. "That's exactly why you can feel safe with me. Both of us know better than to risk a mistake, and you don't have to worry—this won't happen again."

When he turned away, she pulled on her shorts, her gaze riveted on the straight edge of his spine. She understood what he was saying—he'd walk through nails before touching her again. Until tonight, she hadn't understood that he'd been walking on nails all this time to keep from touching her.

Which left her with a question she needed an answer for. Assuming she dredged up courage to ask it. It had been a long, long time since she'd risked anything that could hurt this much. "Max?"

"Yeah?"

"Would it be easier for you . . . if I simply got completely out of your life? Do you want me to leave?"

"No." His head jerked up, although his tone immediately lowered. "I mean yes—when you're ready. But not before. When you're all organized, when you know what you want to do, where you want to be— fine. But until then, you're not unhappy here, are you? It's working out. With Lise. And the bookkeeping. And I think you're getting a kick out of the farm. I already promised you didn't have to worry about me—"

He fumbled around with a few more comments, but Kitt had her answer. It wasn't in his words, but in his eyes.

Eight

Max propped his boots on the desk and opened the file in his lap. Outside, the sky was as solid gray as a painted wall, and his office lights made a beacon in the dark, rainy afternoon. To a farmer there was rain . . . and then there was rain. This was the right kind—no wind, no lightning, no driving force or threat of hail— just a nice, warm, ground-soaking downpour.

It mattered, because he was almost home free. This wasn't the first year he'd had a good season, but there'd been no way to recover from the massive debt load he'd inherited overnight. Climbing out of the red had been a long haul. His bills were paid as of two days ago, including the mortgage; Litowski owed him a bundle and the past two weeks were clear profit.

Max never counted on an unhatched chicken, but for the first time he could taste it. The freedom to expand and experiment without a financial noose around his neck. Maybe even an exotic vacation in Tahiti.

Vacations in Tahiti, Carlson? Where is your head? Max returned his attention to the file in his lap, knowing full well where his head was—on Kitt. The blonde who belonged with a man who could afford to give her vacations in Tahiti. The same blonde who'd prepared this "marketing report" for him to study— when he had the time.

He had the time now, and her file of ideas had him totally bemused. Kitt had systematized priorities— create a market for direct sales; get his insurance programs under one roof to cut out-of-proportion labor costs; computerize his accounting system, because right now there were overlaps; get better daily control on cash flow....

How a woman with absolutely no farming background could be so straight on the mark was beyond Max. Half her ideas had been mulling on the back burner of his mind, waiting for only cash or time to implement, and he'd have listed priorities in the same way. Kitt had an incredible head for business...yet his pride in her aroused conflicting emotions.

When he knew it was going to be a good year, he had to admit that a few wayward fantasies had surfaced in his mind. Foolish stuff...as if his ability to provide for her gave him the right to imagine Kitt in his bed, in his life. Crazy stuff...like picturing Jennifer Lise permanently installed in his youngest sister's old bedroom, like setting a blazing fire on a winter night, Kitt naked and willing and as wild as she'd been that evening at the pond.

Max harshly reminded himself that such fantasies were not only crazy but dangerous. Her marketing report was only one illustration of the lady's business talents. Kitt thrived on being tested and challenged. A country farm would stifle her ambition. It probably already had. Boredom undoubtedly motivated half the trouble she got into.

The muffled sound of a crash made him bolt out of his chair. The crew had been rained out; no one was supposed to be around except for Moshe, and he was behind the closed door of the shop. The main floor of the barn was as dark and gloomy as a cave. Max flicked on a light switch just as Kitt's head popped over the rail from the open third story.

"It's okay," she said gaily. "Everything's fine. Not to worry."

Even before her head disappeared, Max hit the stairs at a dead run. He'd assumed Kitt was safe in the house with the tyke. He should have guessed that a rainy day would ignite her love of exploring. The instant she said "not to worry" his heart had started to pound.

His boots clattered on the wooden stairs to the second floor, then it took traversing an open catwalk to reach the rickety steps leading to the attic-level third floor. By the time he'd climbed them he was out of breath, sure he was facing a disaster.

He was.

"Hi, there!" Kitt said brightly. "I'm glad you're here—you won't *believe* the treasures I've found. Look... and look... and look...."

He looked. He had a vague memory of his father storing a bunch of old furniture up here after his mother died, telling him, "We got three girls to raise, son. We don't have time for anything that takes extra housekeeping." Even at fourteen, Max had known his father was really trying to rid the house of memories that were too painful to live with. He understood, but the house had never been the same home again. His sisters had never wanted the antiques; Andrea had hated them, and ultimately Max had forgotten about them for years.

He thought of his mother and had to smile. Kitt, thank God, hadn't tried to move the old rolltop desk or ancient wardrobe, but she was hugging a brass fireplace andiron with the reverence of a wino for his bottle. And the crash, apparently, had been the result of her determination to dislodge an old love seat from the top of the heap.

"You know where that has to go, don't you?" She motioned to the love seat.

"The brush pile?"

"Bite your tongue, Carlson. It's going right in your front hall—as soon as it gets stripped and stained. And a bit of new upholstery. What's on it's a wreck, but even if I could fix it, I don't quite think white velvet suits your love-style."

"No," he said dryly. "It's missing a leg."

"I found the leg. It'll screw back on and be good as new. Better. Don't you see the scrollwork, the character, the charm? It's absolutely criminal to hide something like this up here—this is the kind of thing that makes a home."

He traced the edge of one moth-eaten, water-stained, dust-coated seat. Kitt couldn't know it, but she'd picked one of his mother's favorite pieces. His

mom had loved antiques, but only the useless stuff—
the things no one could comfortably sit on, things that
stole an enormous amount of space and took a full-
time housekeeper just to dust.

The stuff that made a home.

At least the house used to be a home, when his mom
was alive.

Kitt's animated expression slowly softened. Her
head tilted as she studied his face. "Have I blundered
into something touchy here? If so, I'm sorry, Max—
that was never what I intended. If the things up here
have sad memories for you—"

Max shook his head. "The opposite is true. I
haven't been to this third story in years. I wish I had.
Everything up here has memories—but they're all
good ones."

"You're sure?"

He was sure of nothing when he looked at her. She
was dressed in a pale yellow sundress and cobwebs.
Her hands were black, her right cheek streaked with
dirt, and her sundress was never going to be the same.
She obviously hadn't planned on exploring a barn attic that afternoon, but her clothes hadn't stopped her.
Nothing stopped Kitt when she was running full
steam.

Dirt or not, she was covered shoulders to knees. It
was only in his imagination that he saw her
bare...nubile nipples and porcelain breasts, curls of
pale hair between her thighs and a satin tummy with
just a bit of a pudge. She was so sensitive about that
pudge. He loved it.

Over a week of nights he'd replayed their lovemak-
ing in every dream. In the same week of days, he'd

battled and rebattled the honor of his conscience. A mature woman had a hundred subtle ways to let a man know she wanted him. Kitt wanted him. Some days it didn't seem so terrible to just give in to the sensual tension haunting them both. Same days it made perfect sense to make a memory—something, anything, that he could hold on to during the long empty winter months when she was gone. Some days he didn't give a hoot in hell what was right.

He just wanted her. Kitt had come to mean the sunlight in his days, the promise of warmth after an impossibly long day, the radiance of fire that a lone wolf was drawn to, and dammit, yes. Sex was a motivation, too.

He'd tapped a sensual core in Kitt the night at the pond. There was more there, an earthiness she kept well hidden, a desire she was used to controlling. Max expected her experience had been limited to men like Grant—men she knew were going to leave in the morning. That lack of security was no way to bring out a woman's passion. The right man, with time and trust and love, could have an endlessly growing, creative, thirsty lover on his hands.

And that's where Max always stopped his fantasies. He knew Kitt felt drawn to him, but the attraction was temporary, born—he was sure—from the bond of their first night together and fueled by her temporary need to hold on to someone while her whole life was in the process of change.

So he gritted his teeth, the way he'd been mentally gritting his teeth all week, and tried to think of something else. "Where's my Lise?"

She didn't blink an eye at his possessive "my." "She's with Moshe."

He lifted a brow. "She couldn't be with Moshe. Moshe can't hold a conversation with any female younger than thirty without stuttering."

"What can I say? She pulled a handful of hair out of his beard and it was love. He only took her for a few minutes, Max. Pick up a leg and we can get this love seat downstairs in no time."

"Honey—"

"I know what you're thinking... that I'm going to strand you with a half-finished piece of furniture, but that's not true. It's not as much work as it looks, Max. I can easily finish it in a couple of weeks."

"A couple of weeks?"

"After that, you'll hardly need me around, will you? Moshe told me that the harvest will be completely over in another twelve or thirteen days, and after that you'll obviously have time to do your own bookkeeping. But I can get this done before I go... what's wrong?"

"Nothing." Except for the knife turning in his gut. It happened every time Kitt blithely brought up her leaving. Which she recently seemed to make a point of doing. About three times a day.

"If you're worried we can't handle carrying it downstairs, don't be. It's not heavy. It's just awkward."

"Honey, chiropractors make a living on those famous last words." But he took the front end of the decrepit-looking love seat. The truth was that he wanted it in the house again. The even greater truth was that he could too easily envision Kitt handling the thing alone if no one was around to help her. She was just that stubborn.

"Be careful around that turn," she advised him.

"I am."

"Watch your head—" The beam hit him square in the back of the skull. She winced for him. "Maybe we should get Moshe."

"We're doing fine," he said tersely. Kitt was four steps above him, bent over the love seat. At that angle, her sundress puckered at the bodice. She was wearing a bra, but the view was still delectable—and none of Moshe's business.

"Just one more set of stairs now," she said cheerfully.

"Yeah? And then where do you want it?"

"It'll be in your way in the barn, so I think the front porch of the house. It's not in any shape to be inside the house yet, but there it'll be under cover."

"The front porch," he repeated. That meant carting it through every puddle in the steadily pouring rain.

"Luckily it's warm."

"Yeah, real lucky."

"Max, you were probably in the middle of doing something. If you don't have time—"

"I have plenty of time." Again he had visions of her trying to tackle the thing alone. She would. There was no question in his mind that she would. So when they reached the main floor of the barn, they just kept carrying the love seat through the yard toward the house.

Kitt laughed the moment the first spray of rain hit her face. In seconds her hair was sculpted to her head, rain running down her long white throat and sneaking into her bodice. Her puckered bodice. "Doesn't it feel wonderful? It's been so hot."

When they finally reached the front porch and set it down, she straightened. For a brief moment her bodice wasn't puckered at all but stretched against the damp fabric covering her breasts, while she kneaded the muscles at the small of her back. "Phew. It really wasn't heavy, but that was a long trek."

He was disgusted with himself. Forty years old and obsessed with a woman's breasts. Not any woman's breasts. Hers. He closed his eyes, pushed the damp hair off his forehead and prayed for sanity.

"Max?"

He opened his eyes and felt the doom-and-gloom mood of knowing sanity wasn't forthcoming. Kitt had her arms raised and was coming toward him. He got both a hug and a kiss. A hug where she was layered damply against the full length of him for an agonizingly long two seconds. And a kiss, rain sweet and soft and uniquely flavored of Kitt, of promises, or a yearning that took him out in three seconds flat.

She pulled back faster than a chaste nun. She'd been doing it all week. Showering him with natural and easy affection, none of which lasted longer than a few seconds, always pulling back like that chaste nun.

Kitt had probably apprenticed under the Japanese in World War II, the guys who'd developed water torture to make the prisoners of war talk. Max understood why they'd talked. He'd have given away the farm for the chance of another two seconds of being close to her.

"Thanks," she told him warmly. "Honestly, you won't regret this. The love seat will look absolutely wonderful in your front hall." She laughed suddenly. "I'd better get an umbrella from the house and go save Moshe from Lise."

And then she left him.

Max stood on the porch, hearing the sizzle of rain as it hit the roof, the sound of water sluicing through the eaves, the beat of his heart. This was how it was going to feel when she really left him.

He didn't have to worry about her breaking his heart. The cracks were already there. The damage was already done.

Three afternoons later, Kitt was hand sanding the love seat on Max's front porch. She paused to wipe a layer of dampness from her forehead and check on Lise—the baby was swinging a set of plastic keys in the playpen—and then knelt down to work again.

The scrolled wood was hard to sand, particularly when the sun was broiling her behind. The baby was in the shade and so was the love seat, but Max's front porch was only so big. The sun made a baking triangle where she was on her hands and knees.

She'd worked like the devil to get the love seat this far, but the project was an act of love for Max. She'd rather give him the real thing, but as Kitt was well aware, her chances of doing that were fast running out.

"The harvest is almost over," she warned her daughter. "Once the last peach is in, we're out of a job, out of excuses. I've chased that man beyond any mortifying bounds of pride, contrived excuses to be around him all these weeks, took over his kitchen, took over his house, pushed into his life...."

She crouched down to reach the back of the love seat's leg. Her stomach had a hollow feeling, her heart a growing ache. Once, the thought of her ever chasing a man would have made her laugh. Since the night at the pond, though, Kitt was no longer laughing.

Max was the best man she knew, the only man she'd really loved, and from the first time she sought him out, she really knew what she was doing. Fighting for him. No matter how he felt about her—and in a hundred ways he'd shown her love—Max wasn't going to do the pursuing. Not only was his heart too padded in scar tissue, but Kitt was well aware that the circumstantial evidence against her was pretty loaded. An unwed mom without a job at her age had to look like a user, a taker—just like the other women who'd preyed on Max in the past.

"It was always up to me to prove that wasn't true," she told her daughter. "I've tried, Lise. In a dozen ways I've tried to show him that I make my own choices, that I can take my lumps on the chin, that I'm nobody's sissy, nobody's baby, that I'm strong and resilient and nothing like his ex-wife...."

She went back to sanding, hard and fast. Dust flew in her eyes, but she didn't stop. Ironically, everything she'd tried to show him had backfired on her. All the novice mistakes she'd made on the farm had seemed to prove to Max that she wasn't cut out for country life, that she had no staying power—just like his Andrea.

He was *real* sure she'd never master a hoe in this life.

He was dead right... only the blockhead she loved seemed to miss what mattered. Max could hire someone to do his stupid hoeing. What he wanted and needed in a lover was something else entirely. Or it should be. She thought it would matter when he could see she wasn't taking anything from him, wasn't using him. She thought it would matter that the sun and earth seemed to move, just a smidgeon, every time they were together. She thought it would matter that she loved him. Really loved him, for himself, for what he was, for his scowls and his stubbornness and his huge, huge heart.

Kitt rocked back on her heels and for a brief moment squeezed her eyes closed.

She'd led Max a long, slow dance. And either she'd failed him or he simply didn't hear the same music she did. He hadn't touched her since the night of the pond. He hadn't responded to her mercilessly planted hints about leaving.

Maybe it was all real simple.

Maybe he just didn't love her.

Lise made a gurgling noise and Kitt glanced up. She automatically found a smile for her daughter. Dropping the scrap of sandpaper from her hand, she was just getting up from her knees when she saw it.

The snake was slithering up the edge of the porch to the sun spot not twelve inches from her bare toe. It was a slimy brownish green and huge, with a slithery darting tongue and a tail . . . my God, a tail with *rattles*.

Her lungs sucked in a breath and out it came—a scream loud enough to shatter glass. She scraped her knee as she surged to her feet and snatched up Lise so fast and roughly that the baby let out an astonished howl.

Clutching her daughter, she ran out on the grass . . . just as thirty pickers stampeded from the orchard to the west of the house. Max headed the pack, but it was Moshe who spotted the snake and bent down to pick it up.

"Moshe, don't touch it! It's a rattler!"

Moshe didn't listen. When he lifted the snake with his thumb on its neck, Kitt felt shivers chase down her spine. Next to her, Max pushed the cap off his forehead and wiped his brow. It was only a matter of seconds before he directed the crew back to the orchard. In those same seconds, Kitt had the exasperated impression that he was fighting a grin. "You can stop worrying, honey. It's not exactly a rattler."

"Max, I *heard* it make a rattling sound—"

"That's what a hognose snake does. Makes a sound like that to make his predators think he's a rattler."

She took a breath. "And a . . . hognose . . . isn't poisonous?"

"He's about as dangerous as a dandelion," Max affirmed. "Of course any snake can bite, but when its that young and teeny—"

"Teeny," she echoed.

Gently, possessively, he feathered the damp tendrils at her temples. "Full-grown, I've seen them four or five feet. That one couldn't have been twelve inches."

"If you're laughing at me, Max, I swear I'm going to kick you."

"I'm not laughing at you. How are you supposed to know about snakes? You've never lived on a farm, and even people who do can freak out around them."

"You're smiling."

"Only at the volume of your lung power. Whoops. Not so funny, hmm? And neither is the look of that scrape on your knee. Come on—let's head in the house, get you an iced tea and some first aid."

Max was solicitous and gentle and obviously determined to tease her out of her scare. He made a production out of cleaning her scraped knee, made the baby gurgle and chortle and served Kitt sun tea with a courtly flourish to make her laugh.

Any other time Kitt *would* have laughed. She'd laughed at herself over everything else, but this was different. The dratted snake made it different. If she'd ever wanted to prove herself strong and resilient for Max, snakes were a sure failing ground for her. They'd always given her the screaming meanies and always would.

What bothered her more, though, was that Max expected that reaction from her—and was catering to it. His gaze was affectionate, his soothing ways instinctive and natural. She was a city woman. City women were supposed to scream around snakes. Ergo, he treated her like a naive sweetie who needed kidglove handling, and Kitt had the sinking feeling that he saw the incident as one more example that she was like the women he'd always fallen for. The "wrong" women. The ones who needed him—and deserted ship when he needed them.

His mind, too, suddenly seemed to be on rats deserting the ship. Once he finished his iced tea, he would normally have headed back to his crew. Instead, he perched on the counter on the other side of the sink, leaned back against the cupboard and settled the baby on his chest.

Kitt always knew when Max was going to try to be tactful. He started to say something and then stopped. His eyes worried over her face. He used his thumb to scratch the back of his neck, then pushed the shock of hair off his forehead, and then out came his subtle, tactful best. "Honey, what the hell are you planning to do after leaving here?"

So it was out—he expected her to leave. Kitt felt the blow of hurt, yet in another sense the smallest hope. Open communication had been impossible to pursue when Max avoided any direct personal subjects like the plague. If he was willing to talk, he might also be willing to listen.

"I'm going to take care of the baby—other than that I don't know," she said frankly.

He hesitated, gave up trying to be tactful and bluntly fired his next question. "Then what are you going to do for money?"

Lord, she was happy to get that one out in the open. "Max, I'm not broke," she said quietly. "I don't have money to throw away, but I have enough savings put away to keep us for a while."

"You didn't tell me that before."

"Actually, I tried. I thought I'd told you in a dozen ways that I'm not an irresponsible idiot where money's concerned," she said wryly. "Anyway... I can't float around forever without a job, but we're secure enough that I don't have to risk racing into a mistake."

He thought about that. "You're definitely not going back into marketing?"

"There's no chance of that," she confirmed. "That career was good to me, but I've had my fill of offices and corporate politics. I know what I want—time with my daughter and a completely different life-style for myself. And for the first time, Max, I feel that I can go after what I honestly need in my life. I have time to look, time to make choices instead of being driven by them." She added softly, "You know... if there was anyone on earth who could understand how I felt, I thought it would be you."

"Me?"

"You." She set down her iced-tea glass and drew up her knees. "A long time ago you told me how you ended up back on the farm. It wasn't the career you planned, right? But you were stuck coming back when your dad had the heart attack. The farm was mortgaged to the hilt; your sisters had no love for the life, and there was no one but you who could take it on—"

"Honey, that's nothing like your circumstances."

"No?" She focused directly on his eyes. "You told me why you came back. You never told me why you stayed. Once your dad was gone and the season was over, you could have sold out and left. Why didn't you?" The baby started to fuss, and Kitt automatically reached for her.

Max leaned over to relinquish the little one, his distracted frown testimony that he didn't understand what she was getting at. Still, he answered her. "There wasn't just one reason but a lot of them. The land had been in my family for four generations. I never knew what that meant to me until I had to fight for it. It wasn't that I wanted to make Andrea unhappy, but...I just couldn't give it up. Growing things is what I love—what I've always loved—so much so that it was part of me.''

She nodded. ''So you found what you wanted, you found what you needed to do, and you went after it because you *had* to, Max, even if you were scared.''

''Scared?''

''Don't tell me you weren't afraid,'' she said gently. ''I've seen your books. The risk of going broke is always there. Ten minutes of hail can wipe you out for a season, so can a hard frost in the spring. That's the way it goes, right?''

''Right. If you don't want to gamble, you'd better stay away from a roulette table. And if you're trying to confuse me, you're doing a damn good job of it. You're not a farmer *or* a gambler, Kitt—''

''I didn't used to be,'' she agreed. ''For years I carted around this giant fear of being broke. It took Jennifer Lise for me to realize how silly that fear was. I'm not irresponsible; I'm not lazy, and I'm certainly not afraid of work—there's no way in this life I would ever let my daughter go hungry. And when I finally realized that, it was like someone opened my cage and set me free.''

''I don't understand.''

Kitt floundered for the right words, because it mattered so much. ''You found something worth changing your life for. So have I. For you, it was the farm, but it could have been anything—anything that made you see that you'd taken a wrong turn. Because of the way I grew up, I thought money was security—and that was my wrong turn. The security that really matters to me doesn't even come in that kind of package.''

She gathered up the baby and slipped off the counter. "I used to believe that thinking with my heart was a gambler's risk. Maybe I've turned into a gambler, because I've discovered that's the only kind of risk worth taking . . . and I thought you, if anyone, could understand that. I've honestly changed. I honestly want something completely different from the life I had before."

She searched his face—his dark, mobile eyes, the taut line of his mouth. Maybe words would never convince Max that she wasn't the corporate career woman she once was, but words were about the only weapons she had left. They'd been down so many of the same roads—if he'd only see it. They shared so many of the same values—if he'd only notice. And the risk of the heart she was more than willing to take was him.

"Max, do you under—"

"Yeah, I understand exactly," he said flatly. Trailers were bouncing in the yard. The peach pick was done, and his crew was waiting.

"You have to go," she said swiftly.

"I know." He jerked down from the counter and for the first time in weeks hauled an arm around her shoulder and stunned her with a kiss. A rough, hard kiss that came close to taking her under in a matter of seconds. "We're not done talking about this."

"All right."

Max slammed on his farmer's hat and headed out the door. He hadn't meant to kiss her, but he'd never been so worried about a woman in his entire life. Kitt had gone off the deep end. Slipped a screw. Loosened a hinge.

All that talk about security not mattering and gambling and taking risks—Max knew the life he lived. There was no way Kitt could want it. Nobody moved down from silk and caviar if she had a choice.

And a man who loved her wouldn't ask her to.

Nine

A few mornings later around ten o'clock Max drove into the farmyard with a load of crates. Kitt's Le Sabre wasn't in his driveway. Since the baby woke her up at dawn, Kitt was usually in high gear by eight o'clock—not that she couldn't be out shopping somewhere. It never occurred to him to worry.

The next time he had a chance to get near the house was on a quick trip in for lunch. The Le Sabre was still missing, and a glance inside revealed that she hadn't been in the house. He slapped together a meat-loaf sandwich and ate it on the way back out the door.

Again Max told himself he wasn't worried, but he was becoming irritated with himself. It had always been Kitt's choice to spend the extra hours on the farm. She certainly didn't have to check in with him if she wanted some free time. He had absolutely no right to expect her to be around.

He had absolutely no rights where Kitt was concerned in any sense. And that started to gnaw at him.

The afternoon was a blinger. The combine arrived to harvest a field of rye; that took managing the containers to put the rye into. Litowski couldn't handle his volume of Loring peaches; Max had to line up an extra buyer and the guy wanted the peaches field-run in crates—another management nightmare. Just to keep things jumping, the border patrol drove in late afternoon. Once a season the boarder patrol always made an unannounced raid on the local farms for wetbacks—what immigrants Max hired always had their papers intact; he didn't need the legal grief, but these particular guards were a royal pain. They got out of their cars waving their guns, got everybody all stirred up. To finish off the afternoon, a trailer blew a tire. On the road. Right in the middle of an intersection.

Actually, it was a pretty average day, but there was no way he could make it back to the house before seven. Kitt's Le Sabre still wasn't in sight, but she could have easily come and gone by then. Max wasn't worried. He took the two steps into the back hall in a leap and found no dinner, no note and no sign she'd been there at all that day.

Then, he started worrying.

By the time he had mayonnaise, bread and the last of the meat loaf set out on the counter for his second sandwich of the day, he had the telephone hooked between his ear and shoulder. He got a busy signal at the cottage.

He tried her again when he finished the sandwich. The line was still busy. He tried her again, stark naked, when he climbed out of the shower. Still busy. Kitt wasn't a phone fan. Either some serious crisis was keeping her on the line that long or her telephone in the cottage was off the hook.

He threw on jeans and a black sweatshirt and clamped a cookie between his teeth on the way out the back door. Not that he was agitated, but he reached the end of the yard before he realized he'd forgotten the truck keys. He backtracked at a jog, filched the darn keys from the counter and was on the road in minutes. Although he wasn't familiar with the exact location of her cottage, he had the address.

A half hour later it was that annoying time of evening when the sun was as bright as a peeled lemon and shining right in his eyes through the windshield. More than one car honked behind him, annoyed at his slow tooling speed, but he was hard-pressed to make out the numbers on the mailboxes. The cottage country on the lake was a mélange of landscapes, some heavily wooded, others dune swept.

Her mailbox—leave it to Kitt—was one of the ones buried in brush and overhanging branches. The gravel driveway meandered a long way through deep cool woods, the kind of lead-in where he half expected to see a pricey mansion at the end of it. There wasn't. The cottage was just a cottage, A-frame, white sided and weathered, sitting on a sandy knoll with a crystalline view of the lake.

Her car was parked at the end of the driveway, and before nearing the cottage, he silently walked around her Le Sabre. He found no dents, no bumps, yet his sigh of relief had a rough edge. At the back of his mind all day had been visions of her and the kid in a car accident...and a sick awareness that no one would have contacted him if she had been.

Again he realized he had no rights where Kitt was concerned.

For the tenth time in as many hours, he forced the thought out of his mind, yet he hesitated before going to the door. There could be great reasons why she stayed home today. They'd been together constantly, living in each other's pockets for more than a month. Maybe she wanted a break. Maybe she wanted to soak up sun on the beach for the afternoon. Maybe she wanted to spend a few hours buying earrings and doodads.

Maybe she'd left him.

For three days he'd promised to finish their conversation about gamblers and risks and security. He couldn't do it.

Max would have to be deaf, dumb and blind not to realize Kitt believed herself in love with him. He knew damn well he loved her. When two people felt a matching passion it was supposed to be great—only it wasn't for them. There was no way Kitt could seriously, permanently, want to be tied up with a farmer, but Max wasn't as strong as he should be...not when she was near him. It seemed the height of wisdom to avoid any too-close confrontations. That, or the height of cowardice. And either way, Kitt could have gotten smart over the past few days.

She could have left him.

Max took an impatient breath and strode to her back door. When he couldn't rouse anyone, he walked around to the front of the cottage and briefly scanned the beach. A restless wind was bringing in clouds with pink and purple bottoms—the sunset was minutes away now—and he saw couples strolling the beach, one family with a rambunctious toddler. Lots of people. But no woman alone with a baby.

He turned away and rapped at her front door, aware that his heart was pounding, annoyed that his stomach wouldn't settle. It could well be that Kitt didn't want to be found . . . not by him . . . not anymore.

He was never going to rest, though, until he knew for sure that she was all right. When she failed to answer his knocks, he turned the knob and pushed.

The layout of the place was all on view—one long main room that led to an open kitchen. The basic cottage furnishings had incongruous touches: pink and green jade carvings that looked like a fortune, landscapes in oil, stained glass hangings that caught the glow of a lamp in a sensual prism of color. Max knew by instinct that the touches of beauty were Kitt's, but he couldn't take the time to study anything closely.

Somewhere there had to be a set of stairs to the second floor, because that's where the sound of howls was coming from. He found the staircase and took the steps two at a time. As far as he could tell, it was a double set of howls.

"Kitt?"

His throat closed the minute he saw her. The cedar loft smelled like Oscar de la Renta cologne and baby powder. The crib sat next to an old-fashioned, mattress-mounded feather bed, and Kitt was sitting in a Federal rocker, wearing a giant sleep shirt and, as far as he could tell, nothing else.

He'd seen Kitt cry before—the night she had the baby—but those had been tears of pain and fear. These were slurping, gulping, noisy tears. Her nose was red, her hair all askew, and she was rocking the baby—who was crying just as hard as she was, if not harder.

The noise level alone was enough to scare the heart out of a man.

"Max! What on earth are you doing here?" she said, and then went right on with those gulping tears.

He sank on the edge of the feather bed, dragged a hand through his hair and went through all the rational options he could think of. "Earthquake? Family crisis? Tornado? Somebody die? Somebody you loved got hurt?" She just kept shaking her head, but it took her a while to get enough control to communicate coherently.

"I went to put in a load of wash this morning. The machine—" She reached for a tissue to blow her nose, her voice all watery. "The machine broke down. There was water everywhere. And suds in absolutely everything—" A huge gulp.

"Okay," he interjected rapidly.

"Then I went to the grocery store. I picked up all the groceries; I got to the checkout line...and I forgot my wallet. I had my purse, just no wallet. I didn't have a penny on me. I've never forgotten my wallet in my entire life; the baby was crying; everything had to go back and all these people were waiting behind me—"

"Okay."

"A policeman stopped me on the way home. I wasn't *doing* anything. They were just doing a seat-belt check, only I didn't have my wallet so I didn't have my license. So I got a ticket. Thirty-nine years old and I've never gotten a ticket in my life. Never. Not even one, not even a parking ticket—''

"Okay, okay."

"And then Lise—''

"What about Lise?"

The flood kept coming. "She isn't wet, she isn't tired, she isn't hungry, she doesn't have a fever and I know exactly what's wrong with her. She has a tooth coming in. Only I can't *make* the damned tooth pop through for her, Max, and she's been crying *all day*. I can't *stand* it when she cries. I've done everything for her I know how. Lord, she has to know I'd take arsenic if I thought it would help her—''

It took Max a few seconds for it to sink in, really sink in, that Kitt wasn't dying and neither was the baby. She'd just lost it. She'd had a helluva day and lost it. All this time she'd been sassy and bright through his worst moods; she took on life as if nothing could daunt her; and she waded through every catastrophe—usually while dressed for high tea.

With an exhausted sigh, he waggled his fingers— their unspoken signal that she was supposed to hand over the howling coyote—but it seemed mother and daughter came as a package deal. It was a good thing he was standing up when Kitt launched out of the rocker, because a second later he was back patting both of the bawlers. "Hey. Doesn't anybody want to stop crying around here?"

Apparently nobody did. He herded the crew downstairs, flicked the light switch on in the kitchen and started opening cupboards on a booze raid. He found an unopened bottle of white wine, but this was no occasion for sissy stuff.

Eventually he discovered a pint bottle of whiskey, open about a thimbleful—he guessed it was her grandmother's forgotten stash because it was a rotgut brand, not Kitt's thing at all, but what the hell. There wasn't a shot glass in the place but he found a mug, dipped the pint into it, swilled the first shot himself—dammit, he thought she'd *left* him—and then poured a good slug for her.

He was sure Kitt would give him some prissy objection about ladies not drinking straight whiskey, but she belted it down like no lady at all, making him grin for the first time all day. "Now it's Spike's turn," he said firmly.

"Max, you're not going to give the baby whiskey."

"I'm just going to rub a little on her gums." He was already lifting the baby out of her arms.

"That's an old wives' tale."

"You bet it is."

"I've read a lot of parenting studies, and I'm just not sure—"

Lise didn't care for the taste, but the flavor shocked her enough to make her stop crying. The moment she quit crying, so did Kitt...and that's when it started to burn him. The only reason Kitt had stayed home was because she was having a bad day. God forbid she should expose him to a bad mood. The world would probably cave in if she was less than perky, less than ready to take on any and everything. Kitt never asked anyone for help. She just assumed there was no one she could count on.

The baby was gumming his knuckle so hard she was cutting off circulation. He paced a trail around the living room carrying Lise, and Kitt paced after him with the whiskey bottle. "Why didn't you call me?" he demanded.

"Call you?"

"Call. Dial. Ring. Exercise Ma Bell."

"Why on earth would I call? I wasn't dying—let me try her, Max—I just had my hands full. You have a thousand things to do in a day; you certainly didn't need us to add to it."

While she paced with the baby, he trailed after her. "Nothing I had to do was any big deal, and you two don't add trouble to a day, any day, anytime. Didn't you realize I'd be worried about you?"

"That's pure poppycock. I'm not your ex-wife, Max; I'm not one of your sisters. Of all the women who've ever been in your life, you should know by now that you *don't* have to worry about me. I can take care of myself."

He wasn't expecting to hit a bone. Unwisely, he pressed. "You were boohooing your eyes out when I walked in."

"So? Good grief, I had a rotten day. I was letting it out. That doesn't mean I suddenly turned into a helpless weakling; it just meant I was having a good cry. I *wanted* to cry—"

"Now don't get crabby."

She rounded on him like a cat with claws. "I don't think you realize what you walked into here, Carlson. I don't have to *get* crabby. I already am. Crabby, cranky, aggravated, beat and ready to snap at anything that looks at me wrong, so don't *you*."

He'd never seen her so unreasonable. He hadn't known she could be. He'd never seen the fine lines around her eyes this close, her hair less than cared for and her shoulders drooping—Kitt without her pride on.

His honor slipped a notch. Right and wrong still mattered, but certain primal instincts were stronger. A hundred times he'd pictured her with some good-looking lawyer—a guy with a suit, a guy who could give her vacations in Tahiti and sapphires to match her eyes and so damned much money she could swim in it. She'd never have to worry again. And it wasn't as if Max suddenly wanted anything less for her. It was just that if that exact guy had happened to walk through the door at that precise moment, Max was damn sure he'd have decked him.

"Honey?"

"*What?*" Kitt snapped.

"She's sleeping."

"And in the fifteenth century they all believed the world was flat. We've been through this before, Max. This child is never going to sleep, not until she's twenty-one or I've gone completely gray, whichever comes first."

"Honest. She is."

"Good heavens," she whispered. The baby's crib was upstairs, but she had a white wicker basket thing with a frilly yellow cover in a corner of the living room. When she laid the baby in it, he had to crack a smile. The kid had given her grief all day, yet now that she was out Kitt lingered, fussing lovingly with the blanket, her palm tenderly caressing the baby's cheek.

When she straightened and looked up, he wasn't positive she really saw him. There were soft smudges under her eyes; her gaze was blurry with exhaustion and—momentarily—humor. "If it's okay with you, could we keep arguing? She hates quiet. The best naps she takes are with Tchaikovsky full blast, so maybe if we both try yelling real loud—"

"Sh." The baby was resting, Kitt was beat, and Max's first honorable impulse was to leave. But when he came up behind her and curled his hands on her shoulders, he discovered that she might be exhausted but she was a long way from sleeping. Her shoulders were all knotted up, her neck taut as wire, her whole body as tense as a spring.

"If you keep doing that," she said wearily, "I'm going to fall in a little puddle on the floor and dissolve."

"Yeah? Well, if you think there's a chance of your dissolving, maybe we should take this back rub upstairs where you can crash when you're ready."

"No," she said automatically.

"No to the back rub or no to my spending the night?"

She went all still and turned in his arms. He didn't need to be told that she wasn't "in the mood." He didn't need to be told a lot of things. She searched his face as though she expected to see dilated pupils—some sign he was under the influence. The only influence he was under was her, which she seemed to realize. At least whatever she saw in his eyes made her catch her breath.

"Max," she said slowly and patiently, "my face is blotchy. My eyes have to be bloodshot. I'm wearing a ragbag of a nightshirt, I look like hell, and I've been as fun to be around as a cranky skunk.''

"True," he murmured.

"The night at the pond—we'd had some champagne and it was dark and we'd been…playing. That made sense. If you were ever going to fall off the wagon and risk getting involved, that night made sense. Now—tonight—doesn't make any sense at all.''

It did to him. It made even more sense when he folded her closer and kissed her. All day long he'd been terrified something had happened to her. And even more terrified that something hadn't, and that she'd walked out of his life.

Her lips still tasted like the little burn of whiskey, and that first kiss didn't exactly move Gibraltar. She didn't turn away, but she didn't close her eyes, either. An entire day's strain was hardly going to disappear at the snap of his fingers, and he could see her eyes—blueberry-blue, soft and completely confused. She just plain wasn't sure, of him or what he wanted.

So he helped clear up a little of her confusion.

He tacked a fine trellis of cherishing kisses down her temple, her jaw, her collarbone. Not hot kisses. Soft ones, loving ones, tender, shivery, silky ones. She suddenly breathed out and forgot to take in air. His mouth cradled over hers in a sipping slow exchange of lips and tongues, then did it again. Each kiss was an offer, not a demand.

"Max—"

"You like that?"

Her voice was helplessly low, vulnerable. "Yes."

"Enough to come upstairs with me?"

Her eyes, damn them, shot up again. She still wasn't sure what was going on here. Patiently he kissed her eyes closed and then let his hands roam over her shoulders, her nape, into the feathery strands of her hair. The baby was a few feet away; the glare of a living room lamp shone on her face; if she stepped back even inches her bare leg was going to catch the sharp edge of a coffee table.

It was no place to arouse a woman, but Max hadn't planned that far. He hadn't planned anything. Nothing in his day had made sense without her in it, and that fearsome emptiness poured out of him in emotion. Maybe there'd be no other chance, and he wanted to give her... something. The feelings of love he'd been hoarding all summer, the need he'd denied so ruthlessly, a hint of the passion he wanted for her. She was wonderful. He'd never told her. If it never went further than this, he needed her to know how much she meant to him.

Gradually her shoulders went limp and her spine bowed toward him. Her neck arched, just a little, just enough so he could pearl a line of kisses down the length of her long white throat. He was careful. Decked out in her chains and perfume and war paint, Kitt could be intimidatingly elegant. In a nightshirt with a threadbare neck, she was as fragile as a wisp.

"Max—"

His wisp had recalled how to breathe again. In fact, she was suddenly breathing with assembly-line speed and efficiency, and he could have sworn her blue eyes were liquid.

"You like that," he murmured.

"Yes."

"Enough to come upstairs with me?"

When she didn't immediately answer, he assumed her hesitation. Or maybe he wanted to assume her hesitation. There was still so much bottled up inside that he wanted to communicate to her.

He was a farmer, no more, no less. He was never going to be fancy, never going to be a man to woo a woman with a surprise of diamonds. Kitt was white and gold, silk shirts and class. He was a brass band to her delicate flute, and nothing was going to change if they made love; she was still going to leave him.

He knew that. He accepted that. It also struck him as the height of irony that he'd fallen for the wrong woman—again—yet it wasn't the same. Kitt wasn't like anyone else. He'd never imagined a woman who upped the voltage of sunlight when she was around, a woman who'd seen him at his worst and still kept coming, a woman who gave and gave and gave for a debt she completely misunderstood. He'd always owed *her*.

It was going to hurt far worse when she left if they made love, but hell, he was already dying. He'd held back his feelings to protect her, but to never let her know how he felt seemed the greater sin. And he wasn't going to hurt her. He'd die before hurting her. He just wanted and needed to tell her...

"Max..."

He didn't know when her arms had latched around his neck. She was tense again, but not the same kind of tension as before. When his mouth reached for hers again, she was already up on tiptoe and waiting for him, and he suddenly wasn't sure who was doing the kissing and who was being kissed. Kitt seemed to take him in, sheltering him with her warmth, nurturing him with her responsive mouth, wooing him with her soft hands.

"Max, are you *ever* going to take me upstairs?"

If she was going to whisper like velvet, she couldn't expect him to concentrate. If she was going to rub against him like liquid temptation, if she was going to run her hands up his chest and around his neck . . . for God's sake. He couldn't think. And there were still things he needed her to know.

"This isn't about holding you back, Kitt. Whatever choices you make with your life—I won't interfere. I'd never hold you back. I just need you to know that you can count on me. Even when you're ninety, even if you were a hundred and ten, no matter where you were—if you'd call me, I'd be there."

"I know you would."

"I have protection. I've had it for a week. Not because I was sure of you, but because I wasn't sure of me. So if you were worried about that—"

"I wasn't worried about that. Not with you."

"You should have been," he insisted.

"I don't think so."

"I love you," he said fiercely, "and I'm taking you upstairs."

As if he were afraid she'd argue, he kissed her on the first stair step, then on the third, then on the seventh. Kitt didn't think they'd ever make it to the loft. Her heart was pulsing both tenderness and fire.

Max had shown her love in too many ways for her to doubt it. The difference was that he didn't *want* to love her before. He didn't want to need her. Kitt had

lost hope that he would ever see what they were together... what they could be.

The loft was pitch-dark. Max couldn't spare the
time to switch on a light, and neither could she. The
day had been sultry, but a fretful wind had picked up
in the evening, cooling the loft, making the curtains
lift and drop, lift and drop.

She peeled off her nightshirt. He took longer to un-
dress, but not much. Their mouths fused in a kiss, and
she felt herself sinking into the feather mattress as if
she were sinking down into a wave, immersed in Max,
propelled by him, part of him.

Physical sensations overwhelmed her. The erotic
scent of his skin, the scratchy graze of his chest hair,
the weight of his arousal pressed against her. Max was
a powerful man, and for the first time in her life she
found herself exploring her own power—the infinite
power of a woman to move the man she loved.

Max was naked in flesh, but far more naked in soul.
He hadn't reached out to anyone in a long time. Kitt
stroked and kneaded his hard flesh, abandoning all
inhibitions because he made it so easy. He craved
being touched. He hungered to be wanted. He shuddered for the soft play of her fingertips, but he turned
restless and hot when her caresses became more ur-
gent, more intimate.

She wanted to excite him. She wanted him to feel
dangerous and vulnerable and wonderful... yet Max
tuned in to her emotions and turned them on her. Fire
lapped between them, the yellow flames of anticipation, the darker blue flames of earthy need. He
couldn't know that her inner thigh was unbearably
sensitive, that the bold stroke of his finger ignited her

far more than a softer touch, that her need to feel possessed was as fierce as her drive to please him. He couldn't know those things because she hadn't known. He just knew her.

When he moved between her thighs, there was nothing more hidden between them—there couldn't be. She couldn't wait, wouldn't wait, yet at the first intimate pressure against her, she tensed. It was the first time since the baby. She'd forgotten that. He hadn't. The pressure intensified, slower than torture, until he filled her aching emptiness in a pain-pleasure so intense that she cried out.

"Like a virgin?" he whispered. "They stitched you tight, didn't they, love . . . too tight?"

"No."

"I'm going to die if I hurt you."

She saw his eyes, deep as the shine of fire, bright as the sheen of love. "Nothing ever hurt this good. I love you, Max," she whispered. "The only thing that hurts is that I've missed you. I've missed you my whole life. And I think I might have died if I never found you."

Max's shadowed face turned grave, only for a moment, and then he moved, starting a thrusting rhythm that took them both. The wind kept pouring through the windows. The dark and light, moonshine and shadows, became inseparable from the pulsing dance of love.

Her skin was slick and her nails dented his back when release came, like the burst of stars from deep inside her. It took forever for her breathing to even and even longer for her heart to climb back down from that shivering height. Max didn't help. He kept peppering her face with slow, loving kisses. He kept smiling. He kept looking at her as if she were a source of wonder.

She wrapped around him tight and felt his arms close around her, just as hard, just as snug. She was home. Thirty-nine years old and she'd never understood what the word meant before. Security was the beat of his heart under her cheek.

It was after midnight when she fell asleep. She didn't want to sleep again, ever. She wanted to revel in how good and how right he felt in her arms. She knew every mountain hadn't been crossed. Max had fought his feelings for her too long to underestimate how hard it was for him to believe in her. Love, though—he couldn't possibly deny that again, not after tonight.

Max had simply no idea how tough she was—more than tough enough to move a few mountains—now that she was sure he loved her.

So Kitt believed when she dozed off.

It never occurred to her that the entire world would change by four in the morning.

Ten

Kitt woke in the darkness with her heart suddenly pounding. The night had blown in a storm—no tame tempest, but a wonderfully wild bluster and blow. She'd always loved storms. The fluorescent numbers on her alarm clock flickered, and she sleepily noticed the time—4:00 a.m.—before snuggling deeper in the covers. Half asleep, half awake, she listened to the needles of rain pounding on the windows, the howl of a whirling dervish wind.

A crack and crash of thunder electrified the air, which was the first she realized Max wasn't beside her.

She threw off the covers the moment she spotted him, silhouetted in the window against the stark white of a lightning bolt. He stood totally still, his bare shoulders rigid, his gaze riveted on the storm. Suddenly the driving rain didn't sound exhilarating but ominous—like the pelt of bullets.

"Hail?" she whispered.

His head whipped around. "Yes."

"But it can't hurt you this late in the season, can it? You were only a few days away from being completely done...."

He moved toward her, a dark shadow framed by an even darker night. She felt the press of his lips on her brow, but it wasn't a kiss. It was something that scared her. "I have to go home, Kitt." Immediately he groped for his clothes.

She reacted instinctively. "I'll come with you."

"In the middle of the night, in a storm, with the baby? It's out of the question."

He was right, yet she suddenly leaned up against the pillows, hugging herself, unsure why she was so afraid. "There was no storm forecast."

"That's not news. We're on the lake. Weathermen have been trying to predict Lake Michigan for years, but the truth is that she does what she pleases."

"Even if it's hail, Max, it can't make that much of a difference now—"

"Right," he murmured.

Again, she felt the cool texture of his lips on her brow. Again, she felt fear beyond all rhyme or reason. "It doesn't sound *that* bad—"

"The worst is passing south of here, and the whole thing is going to be over in a matter of minutes. Stop worrying, honey, there's nothing you can do."

"Max—"

He whispered, "Take care of the kid for me."

There was the oddest note in his voice. Defeat? Despair? And then he was gone.

There was no chance of Kitt's sleeping after he left, although for the life of her she couldn't explain her own restlessness. Max hadn't been upset. Max had been cool and almost jarringly calm. It would have made more sense if he'd acted agitated by the storm—any weather made him nervous; he ran his life by weather forecasts, and he'd often made her chuckle because no forecast pleased him. If the prediction was for sun, he needed rain. If the prediction was for rain, he needed dry conditions.

Of course the wind had been something for those few minutes, but the storm hadn't lasted an hour. By the time Kitt pulled on slacks and a blouse, the rain had slowed to a soft patter. By the time she was pacing the kitchen with a mug of coffee in her hands, the sky was clearing as though the storm had never happened. It was still dark; the baby was still sleeping, and she seemed to be panicking for no apparent reason.

The sun slept for longer hours in late September. She sipped mug after mug of coffee, waiting impatiently for dawn. At the first muggy promise of light, she slipped on a jacket and tiptoed past her sleeping daughter to walk outside.

The lake was a murky gray green and almost eerily still, the woods behind the cottage soaked and dripping. Kitt didn't have to walk far to feel the full force of her city-bred naïveté strike her like a blow. How many dozens of storms had she blithely enjoyed? None had ever touched her. She'd always been sheltered by city blocks of concrete; the worst a storm had ever affected her was a short-term power outage.

Everywhere she looked she saw devastation. Downed limbs and branches were strewn everywhere. Hail had slashed leaves to ribbons and completely pitted the smooth bark of a young white tree. Near the road she saw a huge, ancient maple that had been felled by the wind, its gnarled roots gaping from a hole in the ground.

She pictured Max's orchards in her mind and felt her heart turn over. And then she started running.

The instant Jennifer Lise opened her eyes, Kitt had a diaper and fresh sleeper and a warm bottle waiting for her. The baby had barely finished with the nipple before Kitt was bundling the two of them in the Le Sabre.

On the drive to Max's, she discovered that the storm's damage was worse inland. It seemed so impossible. Just those few minutes of wind? Yet deserted cars dotted I-94. Once she left the main highway there was a tree blocking the thoroughfare and another detour created from a downed power line. And Max was alone, she kept thinking. Worse than that, he'd known...and shut her out from any awareness of what he was facing. "There's nothing you can do," he'd said. And in her mind, she heard his defeated tone again when he'd said, "Take care of the kid for me."

Dammit. He was assuming they weren't going to be around.

Police were trying to route traffic off the roads. Kitt solved that problem by choosing a road where there were no police, and when she finally reached Max's farm, she didn't stop in the driveway but kept going down his farm road. By then the sun had risen in glorious splendor, making it easily bright enough to see his orchards...his beautiful, young, perfect orchards. There were tree trunks cracked, branches broken, fruit on the ground.

She didn't get out of the car, but she had to stop. The tears burning in her eyes nearly blinded her. She furiously swiped at them with the side of her palm. There was a time and a place for a good cry. This wasn't it.

She put the car back in gear and drove to the house, unsure where she would find Max, afraid of the state of mind she'd find him in. Lise blew an oblivious bubble when Kitt unlatched her and lifted out the entire car seat. "I need you to be good today, lovebug. Please?" Kitt whispered fiercely, and then carried her into the house.

When she opened the back door, she was braced for just about anything but what she found. Max was calmly sitting in front of a mug of coffee. Apparently his electricity was off, because he'd made the coffee from a camper's kerosene hot plate, and next to him was a battery-powered radio. "Hell of a way to start a morning off, isn't it?"

His tone wasn't cheerful, but it was hardly traumatized, either. Slowly she climbed the two steps into the kitchen and set Lise in her car seat on the table, unable to take her eyes off him. He was still wearing the jeans and black sweatshirt he'd worn the night before; his chin was disreputably whiskered and his dark hair an unruly thatch. He looked like Max—sexy and full of hell—but the glint in his eyes was as hard as ice. No emotion was coming through.

She walked around the table, wanting nothing more than to wrap her arms around him. Suddenly there was a coffee mug in his hand, effectively cutting off the embrace she'd wanted to share. She settled for squeezing his shoulders and tried to pretend it wasn't like squeezing ice. "I drove around," she said quietly.

"Yeah? We won't be harvesting any more peaches this year." He took a gulp of his coffee and extended his finger to Spike. The baby latched on and he smiled. "She slept through it, didn't she?"

"Fine." Kitt sank in a chair, feeling awkwardly out of place and the building weight of dread. It wasn't a morning for lovers. She wasn't expecting pretty words or sentiment—Lord, Max had just had an incredible blow! But after last night, she assumed her right to share his troubles. Instead, he was as distant as a stranger, and she felt as if she were picking her words through a mine field. "Max, I didn't understand last night that the farm was hurt. I heard the wind, but it didn't sound that different from a hundred other rainstorms—"

"It wasn't as bad north of here. I would have gotten you two out of there if I thought you'd been in any danger."

She didn't doubt that, but it wasn't the point. He had deliberately given her no idea what he was facing. "You can't possibly be feeling this calm."

"There aren't a lot of other choices," Max said dryly. "The crew will be out in another hour. We'll start the cleanup, but I expect they're already packing. They know the harvest is done for the year."

"But the damage was more than the harvest, Max—"

He nodded. "Bulldozer operators are going to make a fortune this fall. Luckily she was a capricious wind—most of the orchards will come back; she only took out about sixty acres. So you bulldoze them and plant again. There's no margin in fretting about it, no purpose in stewing. The damage is done. Now it's just a matter of doing what you have to do."

He never said "don't waste any time worrying about me," but his redolent tone delivered the message. It hurt. She thought of all the care he'd put into those perfectly babied trees and hurt even more for him. "Are you going to be able to wing it financially?"

"It'll be all right. Hell, I just paid off the mortgage this week. The bank was ticked—how are banks supposed to make money if people don't owe them anything—so they'll be pleased as punch to have me on the hook again." For the briefest moment he looked old, beaten and worn and white with exhaustion. Yet when he lifted his finger away from Jennifer Lise, the look was gone. "I'm afraid, though, honey—" he lifted the mug and met her eyes over the rim, his tone softer than butter "—that you're out of a job. I can't afford to pay you, Kitt, and whether I want to or not, I'm going to have time coming out of my ears this winter to do my own bookkeeping."

She heard him. He wasn't firing her from any bookkeeping job. He was telling her that, for him, everything had changed at four o'clock that morning. It was over between them.

Max saw her face pale, saw her hands clench in her lap. Spike, ignored too long, let out a little token squall. Kitt didn't look. The whole time he'd known her, Kitt leaped sky-high the very moment the baby so much as murmured, but not this time. Her gaze burned on his face. "So . . . it's all different now, is it, Max? Because of the storm?" she asked quietly.

"It couldn't have taken you more than one look outside to know that it has to be."

"And you want me—us—to leave?"

He'd had ample hours to practice the answer if it came down to this. The speech hadn't been a long one to memorize. "Yes."

He was braced to hear all the things that women say. Didn't last night mean anything to you? What about us? And he was real sure she'd say something noble like the storm didn't matter, didn't have anything to do with the two of them.

She didn't say any of those things, and Max felt the rip of irony that Kitt was the woman he'd lost his heart to. She wasn't going to stage a scene; she wasn't going to force him to be cruel and put it any harder on the line. Kitt had always been perceptive to his feelings to a fault. And when she was hurt, her elegant chin went in the air.

Her chin was high enough to test rarefied atmosphere when she glanced out the window. "Moshe is driving in," she said calmly. "I think your crew is right behind him."

"I have to go," he said swiftly, thinking they'd replayed those exit lines a hundred times. So many times he'd been close to doing something really stupid and emotional around Kitt. So many times his crew had arrived in the nick of time to save him.

He lurched to his feet, trudged three steps toward the door and suddenly couldn't move. She was just sitting there with that proud chin and those blueberry-blue eyes, and she was so still.

"Look," he said, "you can say whatever you want. You don't have to make this easy on me."

"No? I think you just had your whole farm torn up by a storm. I really can't imagine that you need a pile of emotions to deal with on top of that, and anyway...I think you figured we were headed for this point from the first, didn't you, Max?"

He couldn't answer. If it meant his life, he couldn't have gotten another word past the thick lump in his throat. He counted on feeling more in control when they were out of his sight, yet when the screen door banged behind him, he felt a shattering inside his soul.

He strode toward Moshe and the crew without seeing any of them, his face locked in hard lines and his eyes a dark mask. It hadn't been that way at five o'clock that morning, when he'd sat behind the wheel of his pickup and watched the wind and hail destroy everything he'd worked so hard for. Then he'd cried like a baby.

He'd cried like a fool. He'd always known this was how it was. If it hadn't been a windstorm this year, it would be drought the next. His bills were paid; he was in far better shape going into this disaster than he'd been the year his dad died. It hurt and it hurt bad, but he could make it again. There was no doubt in his mind that he could make it again.

Kitt was the reason he was torn up, not the storm—which had done nothing more than make him see reason where she was concerned. Last night, with her snuggled all warm and soft around him, he'd dozed off on dreams of permanence, dreams of making her happy. If the last peaches had come in, he could have banked some of the security so important to her. She loved the house, and there were antiques all over the barns to fix up if she liked those. Lise was a brilliant baby and could easily keep Kitt running circles during the days. Max would take care of her nights. All of her nights. Until they were both a hundred and ten.

It was a euphoric fantasy. And it had died the moment he'd heard the first howl of wind.

Men who worked in chrome offices were the stable providers. That wasn't and never could be him. Up one year, down the next. That's the way it was, and he knew from the beginning he had nothing to offer her—nothing that mattered. Just love. You couldn't eat love; you couldn't drive it; and you sure as hell couldn't put it in the bank.

He drove back through the yard later in the morning with a truck bed full of brush. Her car was gone. The first look of the empty driveway made him feel ripped up and shredded, but he told himself he felt relieved. Kitt was too vulnerable where her heart was concerned. He'd needed to know that she'd finally gotten smart about him. Her priority had to be to do what was right—for her and the baby.

He returned to the field and let the whole crew off. The men were restless and edgy after the storm. One day's work would hardly make a dent in the debris, and he just plain didn't want anyone around. The crew weren't unhappy to split. Except for Moshe.

He told Moshe to leave, too, then ordered him, then fired him. Moshe paid him the same attention he'd pay an annoying mosquito. He stuck like glue through the long hours of the day, saying nothing, keeping a tractor and trailer running while Max worked the chain saw.

Two men couldn't cover two hundred acres in eleven hours. Max kept moving as if he could. He kept moving until a lack of food had his mind spinning, until every muscle in his body screamed abuse, until he couldn't see for exhaustion.

It was better than going home to that empty house, to a kitchen where Kitt wasn't, to a life where she simply wasn't there. He wanted the best for her. That was a rational, practical, sensible *need* for her he felt from the heart.

But he didn't want to go home again.

Eventually Moshe straightened his bulky girth, took a long look at the setting sun and said flatly, "Can't very well run a chain saw in the dark. I'll follow you in the yard and fuel up the tractor before heading out. We're both done for the day."

"Who's the boss around here?" Max demanded, but his voice was hoarse with weariness. "You're right. We're done. And thanks, Moshe."

"No sweat."

When Max climbed in the truck, he couldn't close his eyes without seeing stars or lift an arm without feeling sore. Feeling broody and blind tired, he thought his mind was playing tricks on him when he pulled in the yard.

Instead of an empty driveway, several pickups and cars were strewn around the yard, and his house was lit up like a Christmas tree. It made no sense. When he strode in the back hall, he heard the buzz of voices drifting from his living room. That made even less sense, but the look of his kitchen was the real shocker.

The room was empty, but a delicate rose in stained glass hung from his window—he recognized it—and a kettle sat on his stove. Not a little Dutch oven, but a huge kettle. Stew. Enough for an army, and it looked like plain old wholesome stew but apparently it was going to be served Kitt-style, because sterling and white china were lined up on the table, buffet fashion. Two blueberry pies and a baby carrier cluttered his counter; freshly brewed coffee was on the stove.

Hallucinations, he told himself. But his pulse was suddenly rushing, his heart beating louder than the tick of a clock.

He heard the click of a shoe and looked up.

It was a hell of a powerful hallucination, because Kitt had never looked more real. Her gold silk shirt was rolled up at the cuffs and tucked into black slacks that molded to her slim hips. When she spotted him, her face lit up in a warm, natural smile. As if nothing were out of the ordinary, she rushed over, teased his nostrils with a hint of her spicy perfume and swung her arms around his neck. "I didn't think you were *ever* going to get in!" She kissed his cheek and just as quickly lowered her arms and moved away. "Now, Max...I know you want to shoot me, and I don't blame you, but honestly, there was nothing else I could do about the people."

Max swiped a hand over his face and struggled for
sanity. It wasn't the first time she'd started a conversation that had no relationship to reality as he knew it.
"People?"

"Neighbors—we're having about fifteen for dinner, a little more soup-kitchen style than formal, but
it'll do. I know you're beat and in no mood to play
host, but this isn't a party. Someone had to feed them,
Max. You have your power back, but a lot of your
neighbors still don't. People have been wandering
around here all afternoon—a Mr. Cranshaw had a tree
crash through his roof into his living room, and there's
a little old lady, Martha—do you know Martha?"

"Of course I know Martha, but—"

"Then you know she's alone, and with no water, no
electricity. The other farmers were obviously putting
in the same hellish day that you were, and there were
only so many ways I could help. Running a chain saw
isn't exactly my thing, but there were people in trouble—you all shared the same tragedy of the storm, and
it's the kind of community where you pitch in together, yes? They were all going home to cold kitch-
ens with no power, and the least I could do was put
together a little food—"

She was racing around the kitchen and talking a
mile a minute—a mile a minute with the faintest, almost imperceptible, tremor in her voice. Max heard
the tremor, but he couldn't sneak in a word until she—
momentarily—ran out of breath. "Honey, it's not
your *dinner* I'm questioning."

"Well, good. Truthfully, I thought you'd come up
with the idea if I hadn't. Helping stranded people is
kind of your specialty...." She pressed a mug of cof-

fee in his hand with a dancing grin. If he hadn't felt it, he wouldn't know her hands were trembling. "Like me. Anyway, don't worry about cleaning up; everyone came in from working all day. Just go on in and try to relax. Dinner will be ready in another fifteen minutes—and you have to see Lise. I'll tell you, my daughter's found her natural milieu with fifteen people waiting on her hand and foot—"

"Stop it, Kitt."

"Stop what?"

It was wrenched from him like a tooth pulled without Novocain. "I thought . . . you were gone."

For a bleat of a second, she was silent. "I know." Her eyes met his, suddenly as fierce as fire…and fear. "Carlson, you don't have a brain in your head—not one addlepated, lonely brain—if you thought I'd leave because you had trouble. If you want to quarrel about it, we will. But there's no chance of talking about it now—"

Three women ambled into the kitchen, and that was the last time he had Kitt alone for the next two hours. The neighbors devoured her stew in short order, but then the women took over his kitchen for dishes and cleanup. Every time he turned around, there was an ash blonde flying around, a gold chain swinging around her neck as she poured coffee or picked up a plate. Every time his eyes met hers, she got busier. She wasn't rushing anyone home.

Neither could Max. In times of trouble, people cleaved together—that's always how it was in the country. His neighbors had too much work to linger long, but each had personal experience of the storm, the grief of loss to express. Talk didn't lessen the tragedy, but the power of solace and sharing was real.

Kitt had done something special by bringing them together, but when the hour neared ten, Max was becoming real afraid no one was ever leaving. It wasn't that he didn't care about them.

He just wanted Kitt alone.

He needed her alone.

Eventually they all started shifting toward the door. Outside, Kitt stood next to him, saying goodbye, waving people on their way, but when the last truck left the yard, she'd disappeared.

The kitchen was as silent as the living room, so he headed for the stairs. He found her in the spare bedroom that had once been his youngest sister's. That morning, it had been empty; now it was filled with baby gear from stem to stern, including Lise's wicker basket. Kitt was leaning over it, covering the baby with a blanket.

For the moment she didn't realize he was there, and he just looked at her, thinking barefoot and gold. Stew and sterling. Caviar and shorts. A woman who screamed bloody murder for an itsy-bitsy snake and produced dinner for fifteen easy as a blink. A woman who loved Tchaikovsky and tractors.

Just looking at her made his throat ache.

God knew how he ever thought he could live without her.

Kitt turned and stilled when she saw him, her heart suddenly beating, beating, beating. The hallway light shone on his dark head, but she couldn't read his shadowed expression. She didn't have to. His head was thrown back, his shoulders cocked wide, and his eyes had the look of determination. It was showdown time.

She was briefly tempted to cut and run.

Unfortunately, she'd already tried cutting and running that morning. When Max had called it quits, she'd driven to the cottage in a rage of hurt. Enough was enough. She couldn't keep chasing a man who didn't want her. She couldn't force love on a man who wouldn't take it. If he couldn't turn to her when he needed someone, she belonged out of his life.

But by the time she reached the cottage, she found herself packing the car. One trip, then two. The things that mattered. Baby bottles and Tchaikovsky. Her stained glass and clean underpants. The more she packed, the less she felt hurt. The less hurt she felt, the madder she got.

Max *did* need her, and as for love—the night before, he hadn't taken her in an act of sex. He'd given himself to her in an act of love. The bond of trust was a mountain for Max. He'd crossed it, and *then* shown her the door? That made as much sense as cows flying, so there could only be one reason for his cold rejection that morning. The stupid jerk really believed she'd split if he had trouble. All the lessons she'd taught him that summer! All the humiliation she'd risked! And the rednecked, bullheaded farmer still didn't get it. *Some* women didn't take a powder when the going got rough.

So she came back, madder than a wet cat, to prove that to him one last time.

Only she wasn't really madder than a wet cat. She was scared. Toes-cold, throat-dry, heart-shivery scared, and she had been all day. His standing so utterly motionless in the doorway was only making her pulse skid more erratically. If he rejected her this time, it was for keeps.

And then he crooked his forefinger. "Come on, you."

She didn't trust that crook, so she stalled. "Come where . . . exactly?"

"With me. If you think you're hiding behind my daughter all night, you have another think coming. You're in more trouble than you ever dreamed of, Sanders, and it's about time you faced the music."

His voice was hoarse and hard—real hard when he'd said "my daughter." A slight sensation returned to her toes. Not much. Faster than a heartbeat, he cuffed her wrist and pulled her out of the comfortingly dark room. She knew where he was leading her—his bedroom, across the hall—and unfortunately, the moment he switched on the light he was going to find her overnight bag next to his chenille bedspread.

He switched on the light, and faster than a magnet draws metal, his gaze swiveled to her overnight bag. Without a word, he closed the door. And locked it. Since there was no one to lock out but Lise, the gesture was token, but Kitt got the message. They were going to play this out the tough way.

Her so-tough man hooked his arms around her shoulders, just in case she had any harebrained ideas like escaping. Kitt was getting a lot of sensation in her toes now, and she forgot any escape plans the moment the light caught his face. Max had looked at her with love before, but not like this. Not with hunger, like a starved man who never expected to see food again. Not with fear, like a criminal on death row who didn't believe his reprieve. Not with yearning, like a man believing in hope so hard it was tearing him up.

"Sanders..." His brow nuzzled her brow. "Do you always move in the minute a man's kicked you out of his life?"

"Not usually, no. Actually, I've never been shameless or brazen or pushy around any man."

"Just me?" he whispered.

"Just you," she whispered back. A sharp, white heat was starting to spread through her body—lightning heat—and the burn was intense where he touched. Maybe Max didn't know it, but he was doing a lot of touching. He couldn't seem to stop nuzzling her cheek, her chin, her brow, and his big calloused hands were less than steady.

"You've been chasing me for a long time, woman. But I'll be damned if I know what you think you're going to do now that you've caught me."

Her fingers climbed his chest until she found the first button on his shirt. "I more or less had in mind—loving you." She took a breath. "I think you're just going to have to grit your teeth and bite the bullet, Max. I'm not leaving you. Not in times of feast or famine."

"No?"

Button two. "People don't have to be the same, you know." Button three. "Some people, for example, may never be too fond of snakes. They may never catch on to the color coordination of fuel pumps."

"Kitt—"

She firmly interrupted him. "*Other* people may worry—far too much—about what's best for someone else. They may mistakenly worry, for example, about being the wrong man for the wrong woman—''

She simply couldn't coax a smile. Max framed her face in his hands, holding her, his dark eyes as vulnerable as she'd ever seen them. ''It won't work, honey. Not if you're giving up anything for me.''

She pulled the shirt from the waistband of his jeans. She wanted her hands on him. However warm the night, his bare chest was chill and his heart thudding so hard beneath her palms that she could hardly stand it. ''I'm far too tough—and much too mean—to give up anything that matters to me anymore. If I wanted to give my daughter a legacy of caviar and silk, I'd be doing it. I'd rather give her a more priceless legacy— a role model of a mom who knows what matters to her and has the courage to never settle for less.''

Max was starting to warm. In fact, he was quickly getting the hang of silk buttons. ''This real mean mom sounds pretty sure about what matters to her.''

''You bet I am,'' Kitt whispered fiercely. ''I want a man who's loving enough, strong enough, to stand by me. I want a man who'll stick by me while I grow— doing what I have to do. And I want to watch the man in my life grow—doing what he has to do. Being different doesn't hurt us, Max; it's part of what we bring to each other. And if you don't feel the same way, I'm sure as hell making a fool out of myself.''

Max wanted to answer, and at just that moment couldn't. His throat was too thick, his heart too full. He reached out and folded her close, his mouth claiming hers, hard and possessively...and then softly. Real softly. From experience, he had a pretty good idea what made his too-tough, too-mean woman melt.

Eventually he watched her silk shirt slink to a puddle on the floor, followed by a scrap of a lacy bra, followed by his switching off the light. He felt a little foolish carrying Kitt to the bed. Not too much. Maybe it was cavalier and maybe it was corny, but she was his woman, and she belonged in his bed, and more to the point, it aroused Kitt like he couldn't believe.

Max wanted to arouse Kitt—permanently and irrevocably—for the rest of her life with how much he loved her. He'd worried, so much, about the sacrifices she would make to be with him. She'd forced him to see that there was a different kind of sacrifice she'd make without him.

An hour and a half later, they were still awake. Her head was nestled in the crook of his shoulder; his arms held her close. "I'm going to tell our daughter you chased me," he murmured.

"You wouldn't, Max."

"Oh, yes I would. I'm going to tell her that her mother led me a real slow dance. I'm going to tell her that her dad was a blockhead who was too afraid of losing again. Too afraid to admit he needed her." He whispered, "I *need* you, Kitt."

"I'm here."

"I *love* you. It's more than needing you. I want you to know that. And after I get a gold band on your finger, after I adopt the kid, I'm warning you now...it's your turn to get chased."

"Chased?"

"Pursued. Wooed. Seduced, hunted, overwhelmed and mercilessly chased. When you're ninety-nine, I'm still going to be necking with you in corners, woman. I'm just warning you now."

Kitt cut through his loving words to the rash promise that could clearly have been said in the passion of the moment. "You're sure you want to adopt Lise?"

"Dead sure."

"She doesn't sleep. She cries. She's never going to be a beauty, Max. And I happen to adore my daughter, but I just don't know where that incredibly stubborn temperament comes from."

Max had a pretty good idea.

He could have lost Kitt if she hadn't been so stubborn, so sure, so disturbingly...vulnerable. Hail and tornado winds had nothing on the woman he loved. As Kitt had repeatedly told him, she was tough.

He leaned over her in the darkness. Whispered a beguiling kiss on her mouth. And she showed him how tough she was all over again.

* * * * *

The tradition continues in November as Silhouette presents its fifth annual Christmas collection

SILHOUETTE
Christmas
STORIES 1990

The romance of Christmas sparkles in four enchanting stories written by some of your favorite Silhouette authors:

Ann Major * SANTA'S SPECIAL MIRACLE
Rita Rainville * LIGHTS OUT!
Lindsay McKenna * ALWAYS AND FOREVER
Kathleen Creighton * THE MYSTERIOUS GIFT

Spend the holidays with Silhouette and discover the special magic of falling in love in this heartwarming Christmas collection.

Double your reading pleasure this fall with two Award of Excellence titles written by two of your favorite authors.

Available in September

DUNCAN'S BRIDE
by Linda Howard
Silhouette Intimate Moments #349

Mail-order bride Madelyn Patterson was nothing like what Reese Duncan expected—and everything he needed.

Available in October

THE COWBOY'S LADY
by Debbie Macomber
Silhouette Special Edition #626

The Montana cowboy wanted a little lady at his beck and call—the "lady" in question saw things differently....

These titles have been selected to receive a special laurel—the Award of Excellence. Look for the distinctive emblem on the cover. It lets you know there's something truly wonderful inside! DUN-1

Silhouette Special Edition®

Now appearing
in a special return engagement, Nora Roberts's
bestselling 1988 miniseries featuring

THE O'HURLEYS!
Nora Roberts

Book 1   THE LAST HONEST WOMAN   *Abby's Story*
Book 2   DANCE TO THE PIPER   *Maddy's Story*
Book 3   SKIN DEEP   *Chantel's Story*

And making his debut in a brand-new title, a very special
leading man . . . Trace O'Hurley!

Book 4   WITHOUT A TRACE   *Trace's Tale*

In 1988, Nora Roberts introduced THE O'HURLEYS!—a close-knit
family of entertainers whose early travels spanned the country. The
beautiful triplet sisters and their mysterious brother each experience
the triumphant joy and passion only true love can bring, in four books
you will remember long after the last pages are turned.

Don't miss this captivating miniseries—a special collector's edition
available now wherever paperbacks are sold.

OHUR-1A

Win 1 of 10 Romantic Vacations and Earn Valuable Travel Coupons Worth up to $1,000!

Inside every Harlequin or Silhouette book during September, October and November, you will find a PASSPORT TO ROMANCE that could take you around the world.

By sending us the official entry form available at your favorite retail store, you will automatically be entered in the PASSPORT TO ROMANCE sweepstakes, which could win you a star-studded London Show Tour, a Carribean Cruise, a fabulous tour of France, a sun-drenched visit to Hawaii, a Mediterranean Cruise or a wander through Britain's historical castles. The more entry forms you send in, the better your chances of winning!

In addition to your chances of winning a fabulous vacation for two, valuable travel discounts on hotels, cruises, car rentals and restaurants can be yours by submitting an offer certificate (available at retail stores) properly completed with proofs-of-purchase from any specially marked PASSPORT TO ROMANCE Harlequin® or Silhouette® book. The more proofs-of-purchase you collect, the higher the value of travel coupons received!

For details on your PASSPORT TO ROMANCE, look for information at your favorite retail store or send a self-addressed stamped envelope to:

PASSPORT TO ROMANCE
P.O. Box 621
Fort Erie, Ontario L2A 5X3

ONE PROOF-OF-PURCHASE

3-CSD-2

To collect your free coupon booklet you must include the necessary number of proofs-of-purchase with a properly completed offer certificate available in retail stores or from the above address.

© 1990 Harlequin Enterprises Limited